THE ASSIGNMENT

GODRAK

Ordering Information:

Prime Seven Media
518 Landmann St.
Tomah City, WI 54660

Printed in the United States of America

"I've never particularly trusted mankind in my entire life. My whole experience has proved me right over and over again. How can you possibly trust a pack of predators, forced for their own survival to live together without killing one another? This unnatural co-existence sooner or later would inevitably lead to deviation."

—Malek from "Musings in-between two plunders"

Table of Contents

Chapter 1

"The Wild still lingered in him and the wolf in him merely slept."

—Jack London, **White Fang**

One thinks one knows everything. One thinks all that had already happened has prepared them for what would come next. One thinks everything that could have happened, already did happen, and nothing new or different would ever happen to them again.

You could put all this in three words: A Big Mistake.

And another big mistake – one thinks if they watch Discovery Channel, CNN, National Geographic and Animal Planet, they will be ready for the world out there. Now that's a Vital Mistake.

It's a wonder how such a hopeless and narrow-minded creature has survived all this time, and, even more, ended up filling the leader's shoes in the local ecosystem.

I've been doing time in a strict regime prison for some time now. Why, you may ask. Because I couldn't suppress the animal instincts in me. Oh, yes. People like me belong in prisons for posing a threat to the balance in Society.

On the other hand, the fact that the likes of me should rot in prison is the biggest lie of the ruling circles. They are ruthless and fierce just like me. Yet they never face their enemies, oh no! They send freelancers.

That's the difference which makes me a murderer, and them – just assholes.

I'll come to that later.

I'm all alone in the cell, except for my yard time. They try to separate me from the other prisoners. Why? Well, I honestly don't know. The "Holy Trinity" penitentiary is a place only for a carefully selected group of bastards. None of the wardens, guards, DAs, judges and the rest of the limbs of the law would get a stomachache and diarrhea, if a prisoner gets killed here. So probably the only reason lies in the attorneys who connect the misfits in here with their buddies outside. They pressure the prison chief, his deputies, the guards, the judges, the district attorneys and so on. And most likely they have connections with the biggest assholes in the state – the congressmen.

That's why they don't let me in the yard with the others.

Actually, in the beginning when I first came here, I was welcomed with open arms and great promises. Since all promises were of the same kind and they all concerned my ass, I got bored on the fifth second and stopped paying attention.

I was put in a cell with this big guy, about 6'5 ft. Schwarzenegger would eat his heart out to have any of this guy's muscles. He notified me right away that he was in for serial rape, a bank robbery, a few cases of battery – one of them lethal – and that tonight he'd "have my back door wide open."

"I must've been a real good boy if they're sending me such a tight young bitch!"

I shrugged my shoulders and turned my back to him. I chose the top bunk and put my meagre luggage on it.

"Look at me when I'm talking to you!" he yelled.

I turned around. He hissed:

"You should never turn your back on me when I'm talking to you! Now you asked for it, tonight I'll make you squeal like a castrated pig while I'm doing you so hard… so hard that you…"

"Got a boner already, I see?" I interrupted him. "Why wait till tonight?"

He goggled at me. I gave a gentle and inviting smile:

"C'mon! Please, don't make me wait…" I shook my waist seductively, "Take it out, I want to see it, please…" I drawled.

"You wanna see the Bad Guy, huh?"

He unbuttoned his trousers and took out his erect manhood.

"Not bad for a big guy like you," I said indifferently. "I get fucked only by Really Huge Ones, though! You'll have to pay for the privilege. Two hundred for a fucking, one fifty for a blow-job."

I turned my back on him again. There were two seconds of silence, then he gave a beastly roar:

"What? You little bitch, I'll rip you up!"

I turned round. I managed to avoid the straight one to my head with a bend and gave him an uppercut in the liver. It was as if I punched a wall. I bounced back. He gave me a ravenous smile:

"Trying out for a boxer, aren't you? I'll beat the hell out of you, then rape you!"

I also smiled:

"And I'll mutilate you piece by piece!"

He made his move. I made mine. I cut his attack and parrying his blows in the bud, simultaneously punched a few fists in his face.

He seemed a little dizzy. I kicked his right knee from the inside and when he reeled forth, I welcomed him with a foot in the jaw. He flew backwards, then I grabbed his right wrist and twisted it all the way back until it finally cracked a few times. Bent in two, he started howling with pain, kneeling at my feet. I dropped my foot at his heel with all my strength and broke his ankle. He howled one more time and then sank on the floor and whined:

"Please, stop… please stop… please stop…"

"Serial rape, right?" I cried wildly above him, "Did they scream a lot while you were raping them?" I kicked his ribs a few times, "Did it give you pleasure to torture them?" I kicked him a few times more, "Were there any little girls?" I fiercely jumped on one of his knees, while he was squealing with pain, "Did they beg you not to hurt them?" I grabbed his forelock and lifted his head, "Did they ask you to stop hurting them?" I hissed.

"Please, forgive me… please, forgive me…" he was mumbling through his torn lips, making bubbles with his own blood.

"All right," I said between my teeth, "Just this time." I stood up, tearing up his forelock along with a piece of his scalp.

I turned to the door of the cell – the guards wouldn't dare to enter. They were watching from the outside.

"He wanted to fuck me as if I were a woman," I said, "Apparently, that was his thing. He forgot to ask me what's mine."

"I'll let it pass," said one of the guards, "just this once!"

"Thanks." I said and I meant it. I could very well imagine the tricks they were capable of.

I threw in disgust the torn piece of scalp to his rightful owner.

All of that happened not more than an hour after I passed through the prison gates. Right at the beginning.

On the next day they let me into the yard for a stroll and to meet the other 'tenants'. The event yesterday had spread like greased lightning. There were two groups of people, divided by the effect the rumor had upon them. The one group tried to keep as far away as possible from me; the others obviously wanted to finish what my cellmate couldn't last night. A little punitive expedition up my ass.

Well, the "Holy Trinity" penitentiary is not a boarding-school and the boys here are not exactly prize pupils. They were here because they couldn't suppress the animal instincts in them. And once landing behind bars, they tend to unleash their bestial nature and idolize it.

The strongest beast gets to be the master.

Just like the outside world, only here things are sincere and genuine, as opposed to the outside, where everything is veiled by deceit, hypocrisy and laws.

So, on the next day, while walking in the yard, enjoying life, looking at the others and trying to see through each of them (the brain is to be trained incessantly), I came across a bunch of people, which blocked my way. There was going to be a fight, I could feel it in the air.

"We hear you beat the crap out of Ricky yesterday," one of the men growled out, "He's our friend!"

"Well, yeah, I treated him rather badly." I stroked my thinning hair. "He wanted sex and I was exhausted by the journey to this place. And besides, I prefer a long foreplay – to be kissed and caressed appeals to me. But did he want to do it? No! He wanted to skip straight to the penetration part! Isn't that insulting? I would have felt so used!"

"Cut the crap!" The man interrupted me angrily; he was bulky, clean-shaven and cruel. "I just wanna tell you that I'm gonna rip you up from the cock to the chin, looking you straight in the eyes the whole time! And when you're about to kick it, I'll stuff your throat with your own guts! And if you're still alive after that, I'll spread your legs, just like a woman, and I'll tear your asshole! That's going to be the last thing you see in this life – being fucked in the ass with your legs on my shoulders and your guts spreading all around you! Then, kicking and screaming, your soul's gonna split and fly away in terror!"

His face looked demonic – all contorted, with stretched lips, bare grinning teeth, dilated nostrils, and a glazy stare. His neck muscles were bulging, his veins – pumping. He was clenching his fists, slightly bent forward. No doubt about it – this guy was rotten to the core.

"Can't I just get away with a blow-job?" I suggested, all innocent and sweet.

A knife appeared in his hand, aiming ravenously at my abdomen. I was prepared for it – he had already mentioned the ripping up part. I blocked his knife hand, and with my right hand I punched the blade into his throat. Then I took away his knife and moved around a little. All of his people were holding knives.

Well, too bad for them. If they had been unarmed, I could have been gentler.

I chopped them all in a salami-style. I wasn't even looking where I was cutting; merely using all the opportunities they gave me. Right... I think there were ten or so. I'm not sure how many lived to see the day.

I was saving the shaven one for last. He was lying on his back, rattling in his throat. I managed to crush a few of his ribs – what doctors like to call 'haemopneumothorax'.

'What are going to do if you survive this?' I asked.

'I'm gonna find you and tear you to pieces!' he rattled, fighting for air.

I stood up. 'Yeah, I thought so.'

I dropped my foot in his wind pipe as hard as I could; I could almost feel the asphalt under his neck.

Then I felt the guards' rubber truncheons. I just rolled up and let them beat me. Apparently, that wasn't enough. They dragged to me to the 'Playroom', tied my legs and hung my head down, then battered me almost to death. One of them hit me on the crotch with his truncheon and, seeing my cry of pain, smiled happily. I got a flying kick in the head for dessert. Around this point I had lost consciousness.

I came round in the infirmary. My bedmate was Ricky and he wasn't happy at all. He pretended to be asleep all the time. I bet they put us together on purpose.

The number of people, eager to meet me, had fallen catastrophically since I left the infirmary. I guess it was all my fault – I was tactless from the beginning, so I pushed them away. Only from time to time some of the bigger boys gave it a shot. I respect that – they were the only ones who wanted to communicate with me. But that was then. As I've already mentioned, they don't let me hang with the others anymore.

Besides that, I work just like everybody else – from the laundry-room (one of the easiest duties) to the saw-mill. In the breaks I work on myself. I've made a Chinese wooden dummy, which is now my one true companion.

The more I beat it, the closer we become. That's what I call reciprocity!

Once a week I get to see a psychiatrist – a psychoanalyst or something of the sort. He's trying to analyze me. I enjoy his visits, they amuse me. From time to time I even learn a little something about myself – the man is good at what he does. It's just that he wouldn't tell me where he works. Well, I'll find out eventually

"What do you feel before you give the fatal killing blow?" he once asked me.

"I don't feel anything; I just try to end it as soon as possible." I replied. "Do you think you could become an associate professor, after publishing the paper on me?"

"I doubt that," he shrugged his shoulders and shook his head. "But I'm sure one of my superiors could become a professor."

"Really? How come they get to see your notes? It's you who comes to see the murderer, not they!'

"These are my orders," he smiled sourly, "not my own free will. You amuse me quite well, though."

"Won't you at least get a raise?" I asked.

"I have been promised something like that." He grimaced doubtfully. "You know how it is."

"Yeah, I know how it is. Well, let's give them something, then. If it turns out that you've risked your life coming here, won't you get promoted or something?"

"I have certain provisions in my contract – precarious labor. But I am not the one who assesses that. Besides, I haven't seen any real danger in you, so I'll have to lie on a large scale, and I'm not very good at that."

"Well," I scratched my head "I could pretend that I want to kill you, because you've discovered my deepest secrets. We'll put up a genuine reality show and you'll get to be the Survivor. After that they'd bring me here in chains. Or, even better, you'd have to speak to me through glass; just like that agent did with Hannibal Lecter. How does that sound?"

He burst into laughter. I was pleased to cheer him up. He must have been writing tons of reports in that nasty office of his and kept being overlooked.

He stopped laughing, then sighed with relief, for a brief moment feeling free of the monotonous daily routine and the stressful job. He asked me:

"OK, now, tell me how come a decent wise-cracking guy like you becomes a killer? I've been studying your case for half a year, I've asked you straight in the eyes a dozen times and I still can't get it."

"We're all killers, Paul." I replied gravely. "Every day at the diner, at the restaurant, at home in front of the TV, we eat the spiced meat of our poor victims with great pleasure. And yet we keep talking about humaneness. We keep talking about the starving children and the earthquake victims and what not. We are the most perverse and twisted kind ever to have existed on this planet. At least I admit it openly."

He shook his head:

"My boss would really hate that, I'm not writing it down."

"People are predators, fierce, insatiable, ruthless…" I continued "We do not kill each other only because nobody attacks their equals in strength, just like the wild beasts. They attack the weaker ones, the prey they are sure they'll catch. Otherwise, the lust for killing is there all the time. We just replace it with career-building, sports, hobbies, alcohol and so on."

He was staring at me.

"Since we are forced to live together, we can't kill one another in the open, so we find some other ways to do it. We use each other and we constantly strive to overpower and dominate. The Law of the Predator and the Pack is held good and it determines and defines our whole life."

He kept silent.

"The career-builders are one of the most ferocious predators." I kept talking "Just try to stand on their way and they'll wipe your entire bloodline from the face of the earth! Only they'll achieve it in a lawful manner!"

He stared at me, goggle-eyed.

"And do you know who the worst kind is?" I asked him.

"Tell me." I could hardly hear him.

"The weakest predators, the ones that cannot kill wild animals maybe because they suffer a paw trauma, old wounds, bad teeth, or maybe because they are simply getting older and good for nothing, start attacking people. Become Man-eaters. The man is the most helpless creature in nature; you can catch and kill it easily. And its meat is tender and juicy. So once becoming a Man-eater, you remain one till the end of your days. It is easy and it tastes good."

He just wasn't able to close his mouth. His pen rolled over the edge of the table and fell on the floor, but he didn't even notice it.

"In the Society of Men, the good-for-nothing predators, the ones who can't supply themselves with game, become Man-eaters. That includes all the people, who seemingly "serve" the society – lawyers, district attorneys, judges, the administration, bureaucrats and squits… The scariest and the most ruthless ones occupy the top places – politicians and congressmen. They are the weakest and the most dangerous of all predators. They are the masters and we are their cows, turkeys, hens, pigs, lambs and fraught animals. There's the society for you – a pack of predators, forced to the position of kettle, regularly beaten, raped and slaughtered by their own species.

"But… but…" he stuttered.

"The ones on top are the face of the Power," I interrupted him. "But the real lords are hidden who knows where. And besides all that, in order to preserve this Society for as long as it's possible, they invented The Law. The Law protects the good-for-nothing predators on top from the normal predators like me."

He rubbed his forehead. Then shook his head. Loosened his tie. He saw his pen on the floor next to his left foot and reached for it. Then he shook his head:

"If I write down all of this in my report, not only will I not get a promotion, but they'll sack me on the spot and ban me from practice!"

"If you become a freelancer and publish it, you'll make all the papers. You may even appear on TV. They will probably condemn you; you may get sued for slander. You may be proclaimed insane. But you will get famous and if you know what you're doing, you can make it big. Then you can set your life any way you want."

He goggled his eyes again and shook his head:

"You speak as if I've already done that. It isn't that easy… to let go of everything. My wife will probably leave me. She believes in the goodness in men. I'll lose my job… Besides," he looked at me "I still can't take up everything you say. I just don't believe this. People are not like that. You want me to abandon everything

I've known so far, everything I believed in, everything I leaned on… my truth of life… You want me to leave it all behind and jump into the Great Unknown…"

"I'm not trying to make you do anything," I replied "But you just answered the question of how I became a killer."

He looked at me confused.

"You leave behind everything you know, believe and lean on. You abandon the Truth about the World… and leap into the Unknown… Then you understand there is nothing new. Things are still the same. You are still the same. The only thing that's changed is that you saw through a lie. A Lie about Men. That's it.'

He took out a handkerchief from the pocket of his jacket and wiped the sweat on his neck and forehead. I felt sorry for him:

'I am sorry. I didn't intend to pile it all at once, because you are a good man. But you asked and I couldn't resist. I apologize.'

I don't like to hurt people.

After this conversation, Paul didn't show up for two weeks. And when he finally came, he was somehow distant and cooped up. Well, honesty doesn't suit just anybody. And, of course, he had a wife, a home, a job. Things he cherished and was afraid to lose. I could understand him perfectly.

And what do I have?

I have a wooden dummy. I've been working on it pretty hard lately. I broke its wooden arms and leg a few times, so finally I had to replace them with iron ones. I welcome the slight pain from the impact of my hands on the wood and iron. The limen gets higher in time, so I have to punch harder and harder in search of the pain. I feel a perverse pleasure when it comes to pain.

Actually, it is the only thing that makes me feel alive. When I rub my bruised limbs I feel the World around me is real, not just a figment of some sick man's imagination.

And so it goes.

I spent a year at the "Holy Trinity". In the beginning I indulged myself with the illusion that I may get out some day. Then I got down to earth. The likes of me never get out. Or, at least, they shouldn't get out. The society should not let this happen. It would be the best if they locked up all the lawyers too, so the likes of me wouldn't stand a chance of getting out.

Oh, yeah, my friends, there's no getting out for me!

I'm not quite sure why they didn't sentence me to death. Maybe because of the murder that got me here... there was quite a commotion about it.

In the meantime, they replaced my shrink. Now they send me this cutie in a miniskirt. A pretty blonde with long hair in a naughty ponytail just like a teenager, with playful sparkles in her eyes. She couldn't be more than 32 or 33. She doesn't have a ring on her finger.

Somebody is up to something here. If they are sending me such a pretty girl, things will definitely get dirty.

Let's wait and see.

Chapter 2

"If she's amazing, she won't be easy. If she's easy,
she won't be amazing. ..."

Bob Marley

Even our first meeting didn't go the way we both planned. When I entered the room, where I usually had my sessions, and I saw *her* instead of him, I skipped the greeting part and went straight to:

"Ah! Where's Paul?"

"I'm superseding him," a smooth tinkling voice answered "Is it a bad surprise?"

I looked at her from head to toe. She smiled, stood up and turned round.

"So? Am I good enough for you?"

"Just perfect," I replied "There is one flaw, though."

"And what could that be?" she looked surprised.

"Your skirt's too long!"

She smiled, obviously content with herself. Then she sat down and crossed her legs:

"What are we going to talk about today?"

"Look at that!" I exclaimed, "This is the first time anybody asked *me* what the subject of conversation would be."

I approached her and sat on the chair at the opposite side of the table. Yes, I can see some doubtful smiles on some of your faces. You ask yourselves how it is possible for a dangerous murderer like me to acquire free access to a conversation with a beautiful woman, no matter if she is a shrink or not, no handcuffs, no guards, nothing. The answer is quite simple, really. If you behave well, they don't chain you. If you blow it, you get it really bad right on the spot. Besides, bad guys like to brag about their misdemeanors. They usually suffer from pretty strong insecurities and desperately need somebody to listen and praise them. That's why they do all those stupid acts of crime before they get arrested, and rest on their laurels in prison. They are even proud with themselves. Any smart shrink knows all about it and uses it cunningly, that's why guns and handcuffs are unnecessary here. Well... with a few exceptions, that is.

"Where are you from?" I asked her.

"Guess." She smiled.

"I can't, I'm not particularly smart." She laughed. "At least tell me your name."

"Elizabeth."

"Oh! That name always reminds me of this scary story."

"Which one?"

"Dracula's wife was called Elizabeth."

"Really?" she was surprised. "Are you fond of …such stories?"

"I enjoy a good love story."

"A romantic murderer…" she muttered to herself thoughtfully "Have you got an idol?"

"Pardon?" I didn't get her.

"Somebody you want to imitate and be like."

"There are a lot of famous people I like for some of their qualities," I drawled "I'd like to possess some of them. But when it comes to idols…I think I'm way past this age."

"What do you hate in people the most?"

"Many things. Lying, hypocrisy, triteness, stupidity, sponging on others… I could go on forever."

"Is there anything you like, then?"

"Yes, I said it already. It's Love. Friendship, too."

"Hmm, well then, how can you explain the murders you've committed?"

"I was forced to." I shrugged my shoulders.

"That's not what the experts claim," she shook her head gravely, "They claim you're one of those rare breeds that most people consider extinct. The man-beast breed, which finds no pleasure whatsoever. People with messed up metabolism. Yet in the moment of committing a murder, the production of serotonin, dopamine, noradrenalin, endorphins and so on rises greatly. Then they experience something resembling a religious ecstasy. That's when they really feel alive! These are the only moments that actually matter to them! So they keep looking for them…"

"At least they didn't find me schizophrenic." I shrugged.

She was looking at me attentively, as if she was looking for a particular reaction in me.

"What am I supposed to do now?"

Suddenly, she became nervous. Apparently, she had imagined our meeting to go to a different direction. She opened a notebook with a jerk, wrote something down and asked me harshly:

"What do you feel when you kill someone?"

I didn't answer. She folded her hands on her chest. Then she looked at me coldly and said through clenched teeth:

"I asked you a question!"

"Did you? I'm sorry, I didn't hear it."

Her eyes flashed angrily. She continued dryly:

"Most likely I am the person who decides what's going to happen with you from now on. So…"

"So what?" I interrupted "You come in here as if in a zoo, to see a rare and interesting species, but it doesn't live up to your expectations. I'm not your test animal! If you want me to participate actively in the conversation and fill in your questionnaire with A answers, at least act politely and tactfully!"

"You listen to me!" she hissed really mean. "I've seen monsters that make Hannibal Lecter look good, and you are just a joke, nothing more! You're not in a position to tell me how to behave! I'm the one telling *you* how to behave! If you don't follow my instructions, I could send you straight to the electric chair! A lot of 'slips' happen there! Sometimes death comes after a long and painful time and they have to fry you a couple of times! Can you get that, you miserable fuck?"

I got furious. I tilted forward and spoke slowly, looking straight into her eyes:

"Why don't you give me a blow-job, then let me fuck you hard in your sweet tight ass? Then you'll be able to feel all the hormones I produce!"

She would have killed me then and there, if she could. Her glare spoke for itself. She gathered all her papers in fury, creasing them ruthlessly; stood up abruptly, knocking down her chair and headed angrily towards the exit.

"You're running away because you are afraid you might like it!" I shouted behind her back.

She turned around and snarled:

"Fuck you!"

'Love you too!' I replied.

She banged the door behind her. I shook my head. What's up with this school-girl act? She's sweet all right, but wouldn't recognize professional behavior if it hit her in the head! She had lost it completely! She even got to my nerves.

I paid a visit to my favorite dummy and took it all out on it.

Tired and sweaty I leaned on one of its 'arms' and started breathing heavily. Then it came to me – she wasn't an amateur at all! On the contrary, she was a real pro! It was all well-staged and I fell for it pretty hard! She played me well, I admit it. Screwed me up by the book. I jumped to the bait all right. I was hooked up.

I started laughing loudly. That's just something I do.

Well, apparently somebody started paying special attention to me, if they decided to replace Paul with Elizabeth. Something's cooking. At least it's going to be interesting. I didn't sleep well that night. I was dreaming all kinds of things. In the end I couldn't take it anymore and I woke up. I was turning in bed and thinking. What's cooking and who's cooking it? Who needs me and what for? This girl's visit today suggested much more that mere scientific interest.

Well, I'll just have to see where this leads me.

On the next day I had breakfast in my cell as usual, guarded by one man in front, one in the back and two outside, all aiming their machine-guns at me, safety down. Three cameras were following every move I was making. I felt like a genuine Tom Cruise character!

"Eat faster, you have a visitor." The one behind urged me.

His name was Hank, a 'Desert Storm' and 'Desert Fox' veteran. One of the few who treated me like a normal human being. He even gave me cigarettes and a gulp from his flask from time to time. I once asked him why he was so good to me.

He shrugged, sighed and said:

"I don't like brainless, nasty and mean people. You are none of the above. I also believe that anyone could be driven to killing. I've seen how it works and I've done it many times. It's just that I got some decoration, and you ended up here." He laughed.

That sounded really wise.

After breakfast, again as usual, I had my hands handcuffed in front, feet in chains; they put me in my metal chair with additional ironwork and tightening belts, then moved me to the psychiatric session-room. We passed across the whole prison like that. I was a huge star.

When we entered the room, they unleashed me. Maybe I forgot to mention that the walls were actually fake mirrors. They said they never filmed the sessions but I was sure that wasn't true. There were at least two cameras behind the fake mirror!

I was curious about one thing. The psychiatric sessions were held once weekly. So why another one today? Obviously someone took my case very seriously.

Elizabeth came through the other door.

Hmm…

Olay, lets' play.

I headed for the table and sat uninvited in one of the chairs without uttering a word.

She stood by the door for a while, then came closer. She stood by the table for a few moments, then sat down. She knocked her nails on the table and said with an effort:

"I …would like to …apologize about yesterday."

"Don't," I interrupted "It's all my fault. I was much ruder than you."

She looked at me astonished. Then nodded.

"But my offer stands still." I added wickedly.

She looked at me surprised, then failed to hide a smile and lowered her gaze. She stood like that about a minute. Then she took out her papers from her bag, put them on the table, placed her hand on top and drawled:

"So… Okay. Let's see how it goes today."

She was more than attentive and polite. She was almost …servile. She was trying very hard not to mess it up. I deliberately tried to show her my most wicked ideas. She would just smile shyly and coquettishly look down, casting a quick glance aside, as if she was worried someone might hear and see her act … hmm… horny. Her appearance, her behavior simply screamed to me: *"I want you! I want you really bad! I want you in any way possible1 I'll let you do anything to me! I long for you!"*

I kept playing the game and wondered who needed this. What were they trying to achieve but bringing me this actress? Why don't I just ask? No, I'll spoil the game. There aren't many forms of entertainment in prison anyway. That's why, sooner or later, people here start fighting or fucking each other. Or both. There's just nothing else to do. Well, we have TV and the library. But the former quickly gets boring, and the latter is not available to everyone. Mainly because they think we can't read, secondly because they think we don't want to read, and thirdly because they are afraid we might break the computers and tear up all the books. They are right to a certain extent.

"Tell me how you got here." Elizabeth asked.

"Haven't you read all about it?" I replied.

"It's different when you tell the story," she begged me like a little child.

Hmm, if I'm not careful enough, I could easily imagine she actually likes me and… C'mon! Get a grip!

OK, let's tell a story.

I remember it all very well. They say every murderer remembers in detail his first kill as long as he lives.

I was coming home after a night shift. I was so beat, I could hardly walk. I haven't slept at all and a patient has just died in my arms at dawn.

I was walking home without thinking, my head was killing me, the light was hurting my eyes, and even half a kilo of Ranitidine couldn't inhibit the acids caused by the two Niagara Falls of coffee I had drunk during the night.

My path was going through the university campus. It was about twenty to eight in the morning.

I turned at the back wall of a dorm and almost bumped into a heavy guy, wearing a suit. I faltered forth: "Excuse me." and tried to give him way.

He grabbed me by the shoulder and commanded:

"You can't go on! Go back!"

That was then I noticed the fancy Mercedes ten feet away. Its back door was open. I could clearly see a blond girl on her hands and knees in the back seat and a fat guy fucking her from behind. Behind the Mercedes, five or six girls were waiting in line, guarded by three strong fellows. One of the guys was injecting something in some girl's veins. Three of the girls were holding their bent elbows, swaying a little.

I still couldn't grasp the situation. I looked at the guy holding my shoulder. He smiled as if he was an older boy just finished telling a dirty joke to an infant.

Right then the girl crawled from the Mercedes and started vomiting. One of the guys pushed the next girl towards the car. She staggered, taking off her panties on the way. I still couldn't believe my eyes.

A luxurious Mercedes, property of the state; four huge guys; six junkies, not a day older than sixteen, one of them barfing near the car, the other gobbling the congressman's cock in the back seat of the car. The car, paid with my taxes.

"OK, you've seen enough." said the bodyguard, grabbing my arm. "Forget everything you've seen, it's for your own good. Just bear in mind, I won't forget *you*!" he smiled dirtily again.

That triggered me. I can clearly remember how I first looked at my watch – it was a quarter to eight, and then said absentmindedly:

"After a night shift like that, the day is going to be really hard."

"What?" he didn't get it.

The rest have already noticed me and were heading my way. Such a team spirit! I looked at my guy and smiled:

"It's nothing."

He was just preparing himself for a brain activity, when I hit him in the balls with a palm. When he bent forward, I grabbed his throat with my right hand, got his belt with my left, and placing him on my head, I carried him like a shield. I heard the shots and could feel the bullets hit his body. It softened like an old drag. I kept carrying him forward until the shooting seized. Apparently, the three were shooting at the same time, because there was quite a noise.

After they stopped, I let the body fall on the ground. I could see with the corner of my eye that the three bodyguards were reloading. I gave a mighty beastly roar (quite surprised of myself, actually), jumped on the nearest guy and swung as hard as I could to his neck. His flesh turned out to be soft and tender. I plucked out his wind pipe, took out his unloaded gun with my left hand and turned to the other two. I was smiling:

"Would you mind terribly if I kept this?" and I reached forward showing them the bloody trophy.

The dead body slid down beside me, and one of the other bodyguards dropped his gun.

I smiled again.

"Gentlemen, you are professionals after all! How could you! Snap out of it!"

I jumped on the guy who dropped his weapon and hit him hard on the head with the back of the de-wind-piped guy's gun.

The last of the bodyguards had reloaded and was pointing the machine-gun at me. I threw my gun at him and hit 'the bull's eye'. His feet got soft, so he had to sit.

I heard the engine of the Mercedes. The bastard was trying to escape! I turned around – the car was just setting off. It was a few yards away. I dashed and caught up with it. With a beastly roar I smashed the driver's window. The fat guy screamed and curled up. The engine coughed and went dead. I reached with my left hand, grabbed the swine by the stout throat (my fingers went deep in the greasy flesh) and shouted:

"Get the fuck out!"

The door opened. I let go of the sweaty neck for just a second. I barely had the time to bend – the villain shot at me with a hidden gun. I fiercely pulled the door, managed to escape the second shot and grabbed the greasy fuck by the forelock. He was screaming like a little school-girl, yet kept shooting. In order to hit me, he had to shoot near himself, and life was too dear to him to try anything stupid. In a few seconds he ran out of bullets. I dragged the huge worm out of the car by the hair. He wouldn't stop screaming with his shrill voice and was driving me insane. I kicked him angrily in the fat ass.

"Shut up!"

He knelt before me and lamented:

"Please, spare me, please, don't kill me, I'll pay you anything you want. I'll put you up in a good office, please…"

"What office?" I growled.

"My brother-in-law works for the Department of Homeland Security, I can get you a place anywhere you like…" he begged.

"DHS, huh?" I said quietly. "How long have you been fucking these girls?"

He looked down.

"How long?" I shouted.

"Three months." he uttered.

"Get up!" I roared. (I started forming a habit of it)

"Please, spare me, I'll offer you a sweet deal… my brother works for the president…"

"Shut the hell up!" I came close to his ear "Get up." I almost whispered.

He reluctantly obeyed.

I looked at the girls.

The sick one stood up, came to us and kicked the swine in the balls. He squealed and rolled at her feet. She spat on him:

"I've had five abortions because of you, you sick fuck!"

Then she turned to me.

"I'm ready to testify in court. Nothing makes sense anymore. My parents disowned me; I'm hooked on heroin…"

We heard a police siren and we both turned to the direction it was coming from. The police car stopped right next to us. The doors opened and two policemen slowly came out. It was suspiciously slow for real policemen heading to a shooting scene.

Suddenly the fat guy jumped and ran to the policemen.

"C'mon! What took you so long?"

They just smiled. The one took out a gun, aimed and fired. The girl's head next to me tilted abruptly, then she flew back and fell down, as if in slow motion. The puddle of blood around her head was spreading really fast, though.

She turned her eyes to my direction, opened her mouth and then she was gone…

"*He* shot her, right?" the voice of the police officer took me back.

"Yeah," answered the other cop and took out his own gun, "then he fired at the other girls."

"Too bad we couldn't come in time to save them," the first one shook his head. "What a pity, they were so pretty."

"Well," the other one shrugged and smiled wickedly, "What the hell? It's just some whores, some junkies…"

They both aimed. I was a couple of feet away. Honestly, I didn't know I could jump like that. You could achieve wonders in a fit of fury.

With a single leap I landed on the shoulders of the nearest cop. He was standing from the driver's side. I punched him between the eyes. Landing on top of him on the asphalt, I grabbed his gun, lay down and shot the other one in the leg from under the car. He screamed. I got up immediately, jumped on the car roof, rolled over and attacked the cop I just shot at. He fired but missed. I stepped with both of my feet on his chest and grabbed his hand with the gun.

"Gotcha!"

His ribs cracked and his face contorted with pain.

"I'll spare you only because I need you. Call for back-up! Now!"

I let him go. Then I saw the fat swine running as fast as he could. I lifted the gun and fired, almost without aiming. I shot him straight in the fat ass. He screamed and fell down. I giggled loudly and winked at the cop at my feet:

"Call for back-up!"

I dashed to the lying swine, both hands holding a gun. He was bent sideways. When I reached him, I kicked him in the ass.

"Wow, hard ball!"

He screamed and lay on his back:

"Please, spare me, I'll get you a ..."

"I've heard this one already." I knocked him on the forehead with one of the muzzles. "What I'd really like to do is fuck some congresswomen! Supermodels too! Can you arrange that for me?"

"I could ask around…" he hesitated.

"Leave it," I waved the gun. "Tell me, can you arrange for me the same job as yours, so I could fuck such tight pussies too?" I pointed at the group of terrified girls.

"Oh, that's easy," he started "You can start tomorrow, just let me make some phone calls…"

"Is that all?" I grinned "I knew you were my kind of man! Sorry for being so rude. Tell me, how long has this been going on?"

"Three months, I told you already."

"Wow," I exclaimed, filled with admiration, "Did you fuck them all today?"

"Well, you showed up and interrupted me." He was getting bold and tried to stand up a little. "I only managed to do three, but tomorrow I'll make up for it; you can start too. Believe me, there's nothing better than to get one of those young ones, place her on her knees and do her hard!"

"I bet you're right." I replied. "So today you did three, right?"

"Yeah." He looked bewildered.

"So, your sperm is in all three of them?"

"Yeah, why?" He looked even more puzzled.

"Because in that case, I don't need you." I replied sharply.

He tried to say something.

I lifted the gun. I couldn't stop hitting him with the butt-stock until there was nothing left of his face. Then I stood up with difficulty, threw away the gun and went to the dead girl. I knelt beside her and fixed one naughty curl of her hair. Her eyes, though lifeless, kept staring at me. Death couldn't take anything away from her, except her miserable life. It transformed her beauty into something heavenly and eternal.

I shook my head and sighed.

Usually, I try to prevent them from dying in my arms, so what went wrong this time?

The police sirens got louder and louder.

I turned to the other girls:

"I'm sorry. That was the best I could do."

They didn't say anything back. Maybe it was the heroin.

Or maybe they didn't see any difference between me and the four bodyguards. To them I was just another beast, who just happened to be there and help, nothing more.

Just happened to be there…

Well. I didn't blame them. They were doped and I… What was I…?

Chapter 3

"I don't like that man. I must get to know him better."

— Abraham Lincoln

 lizabeth was looking at me with interest, fear, something resembling understanding and … hmm…wild, animal passion.

Damn, she's a good actress!

She leaned on her arms and whispered dreamily:

"I wish I had been there and seen all that with my own eyes!"

"It wasn't a pretty sight." I shook my head.

"Life usually isn't," she replied, "but moments like this make it a little bit more bearable."

"Excuse me?!" I exclaimed.

"Moments like this make me believe there's still justice after all. Not in court, in prison or in the electric chair… I don't mean that… I mean, out there, in the real world. And not some fabricated justice, but supreme justice! I believe it wasn't a matter of pure coincidence for you to be at that particular place in that particular time!"

"Yeah", I uttered. "And then – here."

"Well, they are dead, and you're alive, aren't you? The bastards got what they deserved, right?"

"Did they?"

"Yes, they did. Only two of the bodyguards survived. One is in a mental institution; the other is in a wheel chair, paralyzed for life. It would be interesting for you to know that after the press told everything about it, none of the survivors' families claimed you liable. What is more, they seized all contacts with the bodyguards. So, both of them are abandoned for life. Cases like that happen once in a thousand years."

"I'm astonished," I said sincerely "How about the families of the dead ones?"

"Oh, they insisted on capital punishment, of course," she smiled "Except for the congressman's wife. She wanted life in prison and financial settlement."

"For that dear husband of hers." I burst in almost hysterical laughter. "Oh, they are really insatiable! They all have five throats and ten asses! That's why I hate them so much!" I banged my fist on the table.

She jumped, startled and dropped her papers on the floor. Three men with machine-guns burst into the room. She stopped them with an abrupt gesture.

"How I wish to cleanse the earth from all of them!" I snarled. "Then I would gladly sit in the electric chair and I'll pull the circuit-breaker myself! It's just that, their kind could never be extinct," I sighed. "They keep breeding, like cockroaches!"

My good mood vanished. It was as if the whole world sat on top of me.

"Hey," Elizabeth called out carefully "Are you OK?"

"No, I'm not. Every time I think of people like that, I get furious, then really depressed. And there's nothing I could do about it!"

I was silent for a while, then added:

"Maybe there's something really wrong with me, maybe I don't belong here. Maybe I should go straight to the electric chair."

She looked down and thought about it. Then she raised her head again.

"Maybe I could."

"I beg your pardon?"

"Maybe I could help you."

"How?"

"Let's see." She started collecting her things.

"Are you leaving?"

"Yes." She got up and nodded. "I'll keep in touch."

And then she walked out.

Now was the time for the return trip to the cell – the chair, the chains, the belts.

At least I have a right to walk in the yard and read books. And most importantly, the right to own a wooden dummy with iron limbs.

It's all good, but it's not how you leave prisons.

Working on my dummy, I make everyone around believe they should never let me out in society. What if I start treating people the same way I treat this wooden dummy? Can you imagine that?

What did Elizabeth have in mind? How could she possibly help me? What could she do? And who sent her?

My head will crack open with all these questions.

I should stop thinking about it. *Que sera, sera.* After this magic spell-like phrase my head felt better and it got easier. I smiled.

On the next day, the guard on duty came in very cautiously. I was reading *'Alice in Wonderland'*. He looked at me bewildered from afar. I put down the book and looked at him:

"What?"

He stepped forward awkwardly and took out his hat. Finally it started to make sense.

"You've been sentenced to death." He uttered. "You will be executed tonight, at midnight."

I looked at the clock on the wall – one of my cell privileges – it was 9 am. Then I said:

"Well, don't look like you've buried me already, there are still fifteen hours left. Any other changes in my daily routine?"

He looked at me bewildered and doubtful. He had come to tell me I was going to be fried tonight, and I was asking about routine changes.

I shrugged my shoulders:

"If that's all, thank you." And continued reading my book.

He stood there for a few silent awkward moments and left. I was still reading. Actually, it's not that big of a book, but if they engage me in some other activity, I may not be able to finish it till tonight, so I had to concentrate and keep reading, just in case.

Then it was time for my 'leisure activities'. I got to the wooden dummy. I kicked the shit out of it a couple of times! Then I took a shower.

After that they sent me a priest. He was wearing a formal black cassock and had a beard, a moustache, and sharp-cut glasses. Standard looking, with an eye for the details.

I stood up and greeted him. He gave me his hand and I shook it heartily. If he had expected me to kiss it, he must have been deeply disappointed.

I offered him my chair by the table, and I sat on the lower bunk of the bed. Since I beat Ricky that very first night, the top bunk was never used again.

The priest was carrying a Bible. It was written on his face that he was here to make the standard conversation with me, nothing more.

"I'm here to give you the last sacrament, my son," he started.

"Does that mean God will forgive everything I've done?"

"I don't know, my son, but by taking it you will express your wish to repent before Him and ask Him for forgiveness."

"And that's all?"

He looked at me reproachfully.

"You can't bargain with Him, son! He is not some street vendor!"

"Then why are you here to bargain on His behalf?" I asked innocently.

He gapped. I smiled in return:

"I'm sorry, I didn't mean to offend you, but it's such nonsense."

"That's blasphemy, my son!" he crossed, "Only if you are meek, He will forgive and help."

"Are you sure about that?" I asked.

He gapped again.

"Listen, father," I shook my head, "Don't get angry, but I think you come in here and speak of things you don't really understand."

He was hurt both personally and professionally. He blushed with anger and decided to show this impudent little fellow (that would be me) who he was (that is – a priest) and how well he understood it all!

"Son," he started harshly and I think a little solemnly (he overdid it, by the way) "God created us and embraced us as His children. We should be thankful for the Divine Breath in our nostrils! For giving us the blessing of Life, which enables us to feel, move, think, enjoy the little pleasures of life…"

I looked at him very carefully. And very watchfully. Then I asked:

"Are you thankful for the gastritis He gave you, or is it ulcer?"

He opened his mouth and goggled. I went on:

"Maybe you thank Him every day for the discopathy he gave you?"

He was astonished. I shook my head:

"Don't look so surprised, father, I am a doctor."

"A doctor?" he exclaimed, "You've learned such an elevated and noble profession, yet you take lives? How could you sink so low?"

"It's a job, just like all others. The electrician fixes boilers, the mechanic – bearings, the worker at the garage fixes cars, and I heal people. As far as taking lives is concerned," I shrugged, "I just had to."

He goggled again. Then he crossed three times.

"Son, you've been led astray…"

"And the right path is …" I interrupted.

"It is humility and obedience before your God and His commands and teachings!" he said harshly and instructively.

"That's all I'm doing, father." I replied. "I listen to Him and do what He tells me."

He started crossing frantically and mumbling to his nose:

"God, please help this poor man, Satan has possessed him, help him, chase out the Evil One…"

That irritated me a bit, so I said:

"Cut the crap! Stop with this fear and hypocrisy!"

He was overwhelmed again. Then he made the sign of the cross and said uncertainly:

"Repent, my son, and maybe you will be forgiven…"

"Stop trading my soul and me!" I hissed angrily.

"I'm not trading, my son," he crossed, "I'm just the messenger…"

"Yeah, right," I said in anger, "and you get paid for it, don't you?"

He startled and froze, staring at me.

"Just tell me, please," I was looking straight into his eyes, "Why did you come here, anyway? To give me the last sacrament or to earn some money?"

He started crossing in a blind fury.

"Forgive him, Lord, for he doesn't know what he's doing…"

I stood up right in front of him:

"I can't take lives, if He doesn't promise and deliver them to me first," I said firmly, coldly and unmercifully, "Read your Bible, father!"

He started crossing so vigorously, as if his life depended on it. Actually… I'm sure he really thought his life was depending on it. He was sitting opposite an atheist, for God's sake; someone possessed by Satan, an incarnation of Evil!

I shook my head:

"Go away, father. It's not your place to offer me a last sacrament, or to mediate between God and me. Maybe to the others – yes, but to me – not yet. Maybe later, but not now. Not yet."

I fell sorry for him. Maybe he really believed in what he was preaching. Who was I to hurt him like that? God forbid, I shake his beliefs a little bit! He could go crazy! I didn't have the right to do it!

Although, if he was a true believer, I couldn't even scratch his thick wall of belief.

"Son," he said very quietly, "You've been seriously led astray! I hope God would understand and forgive you. I will pray for you, I could see you're a good man. May God will help you see the light and make you understand how wrong you are and lead you to Him in faith."

"We are all heading to see Him, father," I said gloomily, "Some faster than the others. And there are those who overstay their welcome time and harass the poor people! These are the ones-" I clenched my fist until it cracked, "these are the ones I politely direct to him."

I looked him straight in the eyes. He wasn't afraid, not even a bit. I could see a mixture of grief, pain, sadness and... love in his eyes. If I strangled him there and then, he would still be praying for me!

"You make me believe there are still good people among priests." I said quietly, "You make me think Faith is still there." I shook my head. "Thank you for coming to see me. Now, go, please! God bless you!"

"How did you become like this?" he asked almost inconsolably, "You must have experienced some great pain and suffering. Forgive and forget. Move on. There is good in life, too; there are many good people, despite all that dirt. You know that, don't you? Look at the good things and forget the bad ones."

"I'm trying, father." I shook my head, "but evil draws me even more." I smiled and went on, "Obviously, evil and me, we still have some unfinished business. As it seems, for the time being, I'll be dancing to rock music, not waltz around." I smiled again.

"I hope God helps you, son," he made the sign of the cross at me, "and I'll be praying for you."

"Let's hope it works." I shook my head in disbelief. "Tell me, why do you think God created this earth?"

"I don't know, son. I don't think anybody knows that."

"Well, I think I do." I replied.

"Do you?" he asked.

"I think it's in the Bible: God created everything, even the Evil one for the Judgment Day." Something like that, right?

"Yes." He nodded gravely.

"Doesn't it flash you in your mind?"

"Like what?"

"Like all of this earth has been created as a form of entertainment. Maybe out of boredom."

"That's blasphemy, son." He warned me seriously, "That doesn't go unpunished."

"Nothing in this life goes unpunished, father." I replied coldly "Think about it. How do we learn to live? How do we acquire our life experience? How do we interact with the world and how we assimilate it?"

"How?"

"Through pain. It is our teacher. We know through pain we are not supposed to touch the hot-plate, to touch the cutting edge of a knife; through pain we understand everything."

"Hmm…" he uttered.

"We perceive life through pain, father. And we learn to stay away. Pain is our tutor."

"What about all the good feelings and experiences?" he asked, "All the good stuff that happens to us?"

"It's only for a brief moment; it's our road stop on the journey. And besides, it doesn't teach us anything. We just relax for a while to get our strength back. So that we could move on."

"Well…"

"Well what?"

"You look at things rather one-sidedly."

"Sure. But what do the good things teach us?"

"Just that there's good in life. That we have to separate the good from the bad."

"Come one, father," I tilted my head, "who created good and bad?"

"He did. And who are you to question anything?"

"I'm not questioning, just stating the fact."

"Hmmm…"

"And even if I'm doing it, who do you think gave me permission to do it?"

"I guess you gave that permission yourself."

"It's possible." I shrugged. "Yet, there are things staring at my face, turning me inside out, and I don't think it's a mere coincidence. What is more, I think it is meant to be this way. The World is meant to be this way – with a lot of evil in it and that doesn't give me peace of mind!"

"Why can't you just go with the flow? Forget evil?"

"I can't do that." I smiled sourly, "That's how I am."

"Well…" he uttered undecidedly, "We should have definitely spoken a lot earlier."

"No, now is the right time. I had to do those bastards in, to be locked in here, to be sentenced to death, so that I could see you."

"Sounds logical," he looked me in the eyes; "maybe you're right."

"I am positive there isn't such thing as coincidence and everything goes according to a master plan."

"And we are just robots, huh? It doesn't work that way, son. God loves us and he takes care of us."

"In what way?"

"By putting his divine breath in our nostrils every day, enabling us to live and breathe. At least that."

"Right, and for what purpose?" I replied.

"Don't push it!"

"I'm asking you, for what purpose?"

"I don't know," he shrugged.

"I know – for entertainment purposes!"

He looked me seriously, "Son, don't push it. He won't put up with you forever."

I tilted my head, "Father, I'm sure my opinion is of no concern to him."

"What?" he gasped.

"Just think about it – He put his own son to the cross, He killed him personally, regardless of the pleadings to "take the cup away". Why would He care about me?"

"Then why did He put his son to the cross?" he looked at me harshly.

"To glorify Himself!" I hammered the words.

"Son, you've been led astray," he crossed, "I mean, big time."

"Seriously, father," I cracked my neck, "I think this world is created for entertainment, nothing else. Actually, there is one other possibility."

"And what's that?" he raised his eyebrows.

"Maybe it was some student's term paper." I shrugged, "I sincerely hope he gets D on that paper. For this is not a nice world!"

"That's just your opinion." He cut me short.

I simply added, "Yeah."

"Hmmm…"

"And what's with the humming?"

"You dwell too much in things we are not supposed to know and understand. Live a simple life. Don't ask yourself so many questions. If it is your destiny to find the answers, you will – not because you troubled to search for them, but because He let you find them."

"Thanks," I smiled, "You should've said that earlier."

"Why?" he was truly astonished.

"Have you forgotten, I get fried tonight?" I grinned.

He could barely hide the smile.

"Son," another hidden smile, "I'm here on serious business, and you're distracting me."

"But I told you I was going to be fried." I looked at him cunningly. "You decided to laugh at it, I didn't make you."

"Son," he almost couldn't hide this one, "enough already. It doesn't become my age to laugh at a man sentenced to death, cut it out."

"I'm sorry," I uttered, "I forgot you don't have a sense of humor." I looked at him bitterly.

He was almost beside himself.

I said, "Come on, you came here for a sacrament, and now you can't stop laughing, shame on you!"

He finally let one smile appear, "You're such a joker, really! I don't know how you do it, but it's there! There's only one thing I don't understand. How can you laugh knowing you are going to die tonight?"

"Isn't that life's normal outcome? I responded with all seriousness, "Death is life's ultimate goalpost, isn't it?"

"Is that what you think?" he raised his eyebrows.

"I don't know," I answered, "I don't know the purpose of life. Maybe the journey itself is the purpose… but if there's no incarnation, and we don't remember our past life experiences, then this journey doesn't make any sense, don't you think?"

"This journey concerns this life" he remarked, "If there is another life, it will be another journey."

"You think you know so much!"

"Yes, I think I do."

I tried a little joke, "So, you probably know the purpose of life, then?"

Getting the joke he replied, "The purpose of life is to live it. To feel it every single moment, in every breath, each sip of water, each hug and kiss from our loved ones. That's it…"

"I think you may be right. I *have been* led astray…" I put my head down.

"Would you like me to help you find the right path?" he asked softly.

"You can't, not yet."

"But why don't you want to?" he cried in pain, "don't you want to live your life in a good way?"

"I do want that! But not yet. There's still some work to be done. If I make it… I promise I will start from scratch."

"What work?" He looked bewildered, "Tonight… they are putting you in the chair…"

"Not everything you see and hear is true." I winked at him. "Wanna bet?"

"No," he smiled, "It's against my beliefs. You are such a peculiar fellow! A bad boy with good intentions. I'll pray for you." He made the cross sign at me.

Then he left.

I was thinking. How sure and determined that priest was! Pity, I couldn't say the same thing for me.

I shook my head and took up *"Alice in Wonderland"* again.

I was a little bit jealous of the priest. He was living in a higher world. A world of Love, Goodness, and Honesty…It was his own world, though. It also belonged to certain poets, artists, actors and … to the people in love…

They just couldn't grasp Human Nature. They were happy and well-behaved. I knew Human Nature. So I was neither happy, nor well-behaved.

I'd better read to pass the time till tonight.

Why was I not panicking, you may ask? Wasn't it a sure thing – I get permanently dead tonight?

Firstly, because if I wanted, I could make trouble and postpone it. I could take a hostage, for one. I could demand a negotiator, a member of the press and the like.

…I could drive them mad.

Secondly, I could leave if I wanted to. Impossible, you may say. My dear, this is a strict regime prison, guarded by …people. Where there are people, there is a weak link. A very weak link.

Thirdly, it was interesting for me to know when and what Elizabeth would do for me. She had said she 'might' help. I was hoping it would be today.

And lastly, the fourth reason … I'll tell you a bit later.

So, I kept on reading.

I couldn't read much. My favorite guard (the one with the booze and the cigarettes now and then) opened the cell door and came in. He stood beside me and smiled widely:

"You have a visit from the highest places."

"The highest places?" I looked at him, "I just had a priest here. Is God next?"

He smiled whole-heartily, "I guess you can say that. It's more like the Holy Trinity."

I was chained to my chair and driven to my favorite room for psychiatric evaluations.

Elizabeth was in the room, of course, but besides her, there were three more men in formal attire.

This time, quite unusually, I was not unleashed. Leaning on the three walls of the room there were three heavy guys with MP-5 automatic weapons.

It felt like the Army. Without anybody saying or doing anything, I could sense the anger rising within me. I could very well guess what kind of 'help' Elizabeth was offering.

She stood up from the chair and came closer:

"Hi," she smiled embarrassed with an apologetic note, "I brought you these people who can improve your situation. You should listen to what they have to say." She smiled with embarrassment again, "Unfortunately, you have to keep the chains on. It's not up to me." She shrugged.

I just nodded in silence.

She returned to her place. Now, one of the three suits approached. He was tall, bulky, with an army-style haircut. He was wearing a formal dark grey suit with a dark tie in some indistinct color. He looked at me inquisitively from head to toe. His eyes were piercing grey. I decided he was a military man.

I don't like to be scrutinized like that. So, I responded with cold indifference.

"State your occupation!" he barked with a deep strong voice.

How I hate these guys, always showing off, feeling better than anyone else. I kept looking apathetically.

He slightly leaned and hissed:

"I asked you a question!"

"Did you," I exclaimed, "I thought you were talking to yourself."

His eyes flashed angrily. Too unstable, aren't we?

"When I'm talking, you keep silent; when I'm asking you a question, you answer!" he was barely holding his anger.

I looked at him coldly once more:

"Why?"

He blushed and clutched his jaws, so that he wouldn't burst in hysterical screams. He fought for control for a few seconds. Then, slowly, stressing on each word, he said:

"Listen, you little piece of shit, it's up to us whether you die today or keep breathing our fresh air with your filthy throat! It's up to us! Do you understand me? So," he smiled and my body froze, "you listen and you obey. Is that clear?"

I nodded. He leaned to my ear and shouted in it abruptly:

"I didn't hear it – is that clear?"

My ears were ringing. Now it was my turn to clench teeth for a few moments. I decided that the dirty deed they were about to involve me in, is over; I'll help this stupid fuck find the shortcut to his Creator.

But not yet.

I looked at Elizabeth. She deserved to be torn to pieces, that little bitch!

I could hardly control myself. I took a deep breath and said, loud and clear:

"Occupation: Doctor of Human Medicine."

The one before me nodded pleased and gave me a little smile:

"Excellent. You're trying to keep up. You'll learn."

Then he joined the others. That was his part, apparently – to crush me and show me I could be subjected to training.

The second guy approached me. He was forty-something, a little bit overweight, but clearly in very good shape. He hair was also cut short, but not in a military fashion. His moves promised many hidden skills. He was graceful like a cat, brisk and threatening. His eyes were… looking for something. I could feel he was touching me all over with them, just like octopus tentacles. I decided he was with the Secret Services. He also leaned forward and examined me.

Are they going to buy me or what? They would most likely sell me after that. That's okay; it's even more interesting that way!

The second man nodded to himself, as if he was happy with the examination. He stood up and returned to the others, without uttering a word.

The third one didn't come at all. In return, he spoke. Finally someone was acting normally!

"As you already know," he started, "we can offer you a complete pardon before the state and laws."

I nodded silently.

"In return, we want you to do something."

I nodded again.

"After completing the assignment, we offer you a new identity and a new life, far away from here."

Another nod.

"Let me tell you this, though," he changed slightly his intonation into a threatening one, "if you decide to run away, not to obey, to harm us in any way, we will shoot you on the spot, even in the back, if necessary." he shrugged. "If I may put it this way, we'll forget you ever existed."

He looked at me with his watery grayish-blue eyes, "Do you understand?"

Again, I just nodded in silence.

"Good, I'm glad we're unanimous on that."

The free of them stood up and walked out of the door. Elizabeth approached me hesitantly. Without looking, she said embarrassed:

"I'm really sorry to put you into this, but there wasn't any other way! If you hadn't agreed to do the assignment, you would have died in the electric chair tonight!"

I nodded.

As she standing before me in her miniskirt, she leaned and kissed me on the left cheek. Then she turned around and almost ran away of the room.

I clenched my teeth.

One of the armed guards gave a whistle, "Gee, bro, I almost wished I was chained and sentenced!"

"Be careful what you wish for," I said quietly.

He startled. He looked at me frightened, although he had a gun in his hands. Obviously, I had used my 'mean' voice.

They came to drag me out of the room. When I was back and free in my cell, I asked the guard for a cigarette. I usually smoke when I'm down or really angry. Now I was simply furious! What do these three assholes think they were? The Father, the Son, and the Holy Spirit?

I finished my smoke, got up and beat the crap out of my dummy.

Then I sat and started thinking about it. I had a choice. If I say 'No' to the blockheads, I go in the electric chair tonight. If I say 'Yes', I have to get involved in whatever nasty business they had in mind. It was very probable I could get killed afterwards. It seemed I found the electric chair more welcoming.

I have no spy training; I have… no training at all. I couldn't survive an hour, surrounded by secret agents and professional assassins. That suggested my assignment couldn't be that hard, because I'm a simple guy. It's probably something stupid. To shoot some senator on the square, for example, right before the eyes of the journalists. Then take the blame for it.

It's all the same, it seems.

But…

I'm getting my plug pulled at midnight. *Finito*, the end. Unless I decided to escape. But I didn't feel like escaping. I was feeling lazy. Wasn't up to it.

Those guys were at least offering some exciting adventure. Maybe even a new life, although that was quite doubtful. I was supposed to be grateful to them, wasn't I?

On the other hand, I have nothing to live for… why not end it tonight? Let them go to hell! I'll be dead anyway.

Okay, I've decided. I have nothing to lose. I will take the assignment, because it might be fun. Good.

I grabbed *"Alice in Wonderland"* and went on reading.

Nothing happened till the evening. Absolutely nothing. Since it was officially my last day, they freed me of all my duties. They even served me lunch in my cell, then dinner, worthy of a five-star hotel! Even a bottle of 'Jack Daniels', imagine that! I exclaimed happily:

"Hey, boys, why didn't you sentence me earlier, so I could see you had a style!"

"Eat faster, you haven't got much time left!" one of the nastiest guards interrupted me, "You may not get to digest the meal." he smiled really ugly.

"One could never know which one of us will live longer." I looked at him coldly.

He quickly backed up a few feet. I saluted him with a glass of bourbon and sipped.

In the evening the priest came again. Apparently, he really wanted to help. I got up and greeted him. Again, I didn't kiss his hand. I offered him my chair one more time. I poured him some bourbon and returned to my bunk.

"Are you ready for your last sacrament, my son?" he asked gently.

"Look now," I replied, "first of all, I don't really believe I need to have a last sacrament."

He shook his head. Obviously, I hadn't repented.

"You weren't present at my birth; I don't see why you should bother to send me off." I explained. "Do you know by any chance where I am going?"

I startled him again, but he contented with a simple head shake.

"I think we simply need to have somebody around, when we go, because we are terrified of the unknown. We're just dying of fear. And it hurts, which increases our fear. Can you tell me why God made us agonize? Who needs us to shrivel from pain, when we know our life is almost over?"

"I don't know, son." he shook his head, "I'm not sure anyone can answer that for you."

"Anyway, thank you for bothering to see me again. You are a good and kind person."

He looked at me in surprise.

"You didn't make me commit sins or stupid things," I went on, "Nor do you have the power to pardon me and take way my sins. You know, there is only One who does that. But I enjoy your company, anyway."

He sipped thoughtfully.

"Besides," I added, "What will happen if you gave me the last sacrament now, and they decided to pardon me and set me free tonight?"

"You don't really believe that's going to happen, do you?" He sipped again, "But if it did, you could start a new life, start over from a scratch."

"From a scratch…" I uttered, "I don't know what "from a scratch" means, but thanks for your advice. I'll take it into consideration, if I can."

He nodded, finished his bourbon and got up. I also rose:

"Thank you again," I reached and grabbed his hand, "It was a pleasure, really."

He hesitated, but lifted his hand and crossed me. Then he said sadly:

"Goodbye, my son."

And he was gone.

I shouted after him, "I'll start from a scratch, I promise."

I wanted him to have hopes for me.

And there I was, wrapped in my thoughts. I couldn't stop pondering, no matter how hard I tried.

Half an hour before my execution time I was given clean new clothes. Quite plain and ordinary, yet new and unused.

So I wasn't going to participate in anything interesting. There wasn't going to be a new life from a scratch. So the three guys Elizabeth brought couldn't stop the execution. That meant I'd be dead in half an hour. They were going to strap me in the electric chair and fry me to death. So... that was it.

What's past is past; I was going to die that night.

Okay, then.

It was just Option B, what's the big deal?

Chapter 4

"You have to die a few times before you can really live."

— Charles Bukowski

I didn't hurry while I was changing my clothes. I didn't shave – I didn't have a date. At least not with someone I cared about. It was all the same to the electric chair.

Later they apologized and trapped me to my wheel chair. I let them do it. Nothing mattered anymore.

They drove me to the Chair. It was in a large room on the first floor of the central prison building. As you remember, I was stationed in the west wing. Which meant we had to pass across half of the prison. This meant I heard quite a lot of things, while they were pushing me along the bars. Most of it, surprisingly, was pep-talk and good-luck wishes. A couple of men wanted to fuck me hard, for the last time. Well, it's true that my butt is round, hard, tight and pretty attractive. If I could, I would fuck myself with great pleasure! So, I wasn't cross with them.

There was this idiot, though, who was jumping in his cell when we were passing by. He was screaming at us, "Why did you chain him for? Give him to me; I'll spare you the electricity bill! Give him to me! Why, you're acting as a real criminal now, you stupid fuck? Come here, you cocksucker!"

"What is he in for?" I asked one of the guards.

"He's a rapist, a pimp and a dealer," the guard replied disgusted, "His lawyers keep appealing like crazy. He gets the death penalty every other month, but he's going to live, that son of a bitch!"

"Could you stop so I could say a few words to him?"

He looked at his watch. The guards exchanged glances. They nodded to each other. Then they turned the wheel-chair round and moved me back in front of the guy's cell. They put me down, facing the cell.

The guy went nuts. He couldn't stand still. He didn't even listen to what he was screaming. Just like a monkey.

I asked him calmly:

"This stinks, huh?"

He didn't hear me and continued jumping around.

"It stinks to be in a cell, and your lawyers to be outside doing whatever they like and just living their lives."

He stopped and looked at me.

"You used to be the King of the block, now you're just another inmate."

"You know nothing about me, you piece of shit!" he was screaming, "Give him to me and I'll get rid of him!"

"To tell you honestly," I went on, as if nothing happened, "If I were you, I would go crazy, too."

He pressed himself hard to the bars.

"To know how much money I waste every day on those who don't even visit me." I said quietly, "To know that my life is passing me by in that little cell, and in the same time, they are driving their expensive limousines, eating in fancy restaurants, sleeping with supermodels. With my own money! And they don't really care if they could postpone my death sentence. For I have already paid them. Maybe I even paid for a year in advance. And if I get fried in the chair, they'll just find somebody else to feed on."

"Take him away! He cried, 'Take him away!"

"And the worst part is," I continued coldly, "that you've always led a life like this – behind two by two bars! Long before you ended up in prison. Ever since you were a small-time dealer, you've been thinking only about how to sell the stuff as fast as you can and get away from somebody else's territory. You were thinking only about survival. Life in a two by two cell! Then, when you've risen up in the world and started conquering your own territories, you kept living in a cell. You were constantly watching your back. You didn't have time to actually live. You didn't have the privilege of having a personal life. You lived in a two by two cell. All women you fucked saw you as just another pig they could feed on. They lied to you every time they could. And you trusted them. You've been living in a two by two cell."

He was staring at me in silence.

"Honestly speaking," I went on, "you lived for the benefit of Society, without getting anything in return. If someone needs drugs, you supply. If somebody wants whores, you deliver. All the time watching your back. No pleasure, no joy! And in the end? A two by two cell and the death sentences keep coming. The lawyers you pay get laid with your money! That's your life! My dear," I shook my head, "you were just doing what you were told. Now it's a matter of time for your lawyers to get a larger sum from somebody else and to forget you. That's your life – two by two."

He was just staring in silence. I decided to finish him off, because the guards were getting impatient – my sentence was waiting, too.

"The saddest thing of all," I added, "is that you never felt the true simple human pleasures. Love, joy, friendship... And you never will! You never had a personal life! And you never will! You've never been happy!" I paused, "And you never will be!" I shook my head, "Your whole life was just a two by two cell! And if I were you, I would kill myself and end this farce!"

I looked at the guard on my right:

"Let's move it, we're late!"

He shook his head (What a freak!). Then he took me to the Chair. It felt like such a long time. I wanted to end it as quickly as possible. Why wait?

At last I saw the big room with the Chair in the middle. With the big fake mirror opposite the Chair, with three rows of chairs behind it for the Show's Special guests!

We, the people, have always been keenly interested in death. That's normal – it is exciting, important and terrifying after all. But I can't understand the interest some of us have in Life's final manifestations in a dying creature. Saliva, vomiting, shitting oneself, pissing all over... the agony, the suffering, the deathly wheezing, the pain and terror on one's face!!!

Especially when you are hurting them deliberately!!!

That's so twisted that I can't accept it!

Yet, there are always viewers behind the fake mirror. Sometimes, they are decent-looking men and women. Yeah. There isn't a more deceitful, lying and hypocritical creature than Man!

They pushed me into the room. There were three guards with guns. Just a precaution. In case I decide to snap someone's neck in the last moment (Truth be told, I suddenly felt the urge to do it and browsed through the people present; the armed boy on my right could come in handy; after I had my handcuffs removed, I could jump behind the chair, nice and easy, and harvest some innocent lives for the last time. I gave up the idea – I was waiting to see what Elizabeth and her wicked companions would do).

Very carefully, quite kind-heartedly, they let me out of the chains and led me to the Chair. I was walking without a care in this world. There was no need to hurry. That was, most likely, my last walk on this earth. I felt a cracking pain in my left knee. Hmmm…

When you know you're losing something, you remember every detail about it. When you retire, you remember all your colleagues with all their peculiarities – a smile, a bald spot, clothing fashions, smell (if any), the blowing of noses, the leg crossing… the warm or the lifeless dough-like handshake… When you leave the house you were living in, you remember everything – the barely visible cracks on the walls, the scratched wallpapers in the kitchen, the fallen plastering in the bathroom… the sweet bent gutter at the eaves' corner… When someone close to you is passing away, they sink into the memory as a last-minute snapshot. A look, an expression, breathing, last words…

When you leave life, especially if you're conscious; you try, quite involuntarily, to pile up some vivid and bright memories.

You never know if you're going to need them in future.

They gently helped me climb on the Chair. Very carefully, almost tenderly, they tightened all the belts, so that I couldn't twitch a muscle.

And then the Priest arrived again.

"Father," I said, "You work too much. That's an ungrateful kind of job and doesn't become you. Why don't you become a kindergarten teacher?"

He gave me a little smile, crossed me, and went out without a word.

One of the guards stood before me:

"Any last words?"

"Yeah, could you move, please, I'd like to talk to the audience."

He smiled faintly and moved.

I stared at the mirror, occupying the whole opposite wall and started slowly. This might have as well been my last reasonable act, so I wanted to do it the right way.

"Thank you all for coming," I started politely, "and yet, I would've been happier, if you were standing where I could see you, too. What you're doing now resembles the time you rented a porn movie and were scared shitless that your parents might catch you watching. I honestly don't understand why you make such a big deal of one man's frying to death? I wouldn't stick around and watch. When I killed someone, I never did it with pleasure and joy, as you are doing now. That makes you perverts and me – far more normal than anybody else here. I guess, if you lived ages ago, you would be members of the Holy Inquisition," I gulped and continued, "Killing doesn't make me feel like God. I think, however, you're all playing God here. What you need is urgent and long psychiatric treatment!"

I glanced at the nearest guard:

"Get on with it!"

He looked at me in dismay. Wasn't I going to beg for mercy? Shouldn't I repent? Won't I kick and scream? Won't I promise to reform, if only they pardon me? Wasn't there going to be any emotion?!

Just as any other normal person...

What was I thinking, what was I feeling inside?

Well, to begin with, I sensed sharply everything that was going on around me. I could see everything and everybody crystal clear and to the smallest detail. I could hear the slightest noise. I smelled a whole bouquet of scents...

I tried to remember that part.

I could also sense fear. A strong smell of Great Fear. The guards were afraid of me. Why? It's simple. Because I wasn't afraid either of them or of the Chair.

If it was up to me, I would die lying on a fresh forest glade. Trees, grass, birds, flowers, vermin… Life! A sense of Life!

Well, it's not up to me.

With my peripheral vision I saw one of the guards grabbing the circuit-breaker.

They put the wet with electrolytic liquid sponge on my head, so that my brain gets fried well. Then, they put the iron helmet on and fastened it with the leashes.

Oh, well, that was it…

I closed my eyes, relaxed and said quietly to myself, "Take me, God."

Chapter 5

othing happened for about a minute. I decided to wait a little longer.

Am I dead? I didn't feel anything. There was no pain, no agony... nothing like that.

Obviously, they hadn't pulled the plug yet. I won't open my eyes.

Someone started loosening the helmet belts. I cast a quick glance. One of the guards was taking it off.

"What's going on?" I asked, "Did the electricity get more expensive all of a sudden?"

"You've been pardoned," he replied and continued loosening all the belts.

Elizabeth stood before me and showed me an Order for Pardon by Whoever. She was beaming with joy. She expected me to jump from happiness, too.

"What's up?" I decided to take a shot at her as well.

"You've been pardoned." She twittered.

Oh, how sweet and innocent of her! I have to say something nice to participate in the game.

"Thank you," I closed my eyes and took a deep breath, then exhaled noisily and looked at her, "Thank you!"

She just smiled.

I didn't know how to pretend better, so I just thanked and took another deep breath. Obviously, it does the trick and mimics relief.

I looked at the wall to wall mirror on the opposite wall and … suddenly something happened to me… I could see all the people standing behind it! All of them! Five men and four women. I could see them to the last detail – who was wearing what, who was sitting where and how exactly, who was wearing make-up and what kind, even what perfumes they were wearing…(I could smell all of them) … and also… who was feeling what to the last drop of emotion!

They were all sitting in the front row. (That's too bad - too few people for a great ego like mine!) First, from left to right, was this man in his fifties. Brown checked suit. Thick, brown and yellow checked tie. Light blue shirt, perfectly matching the suit and the tie. Dark brown shoes. Light brown socks. Nice haircut, combed to the left, though. But it complemented his blue eyes. He was showing marked interest whether I had done number one or number two in my pants. He was gulping nervously; breathing with difficulty, his left hand was resting on his crotch. That man was a district court judge.

Then there was this youngster not a day older than 23 or 24. He was dressed casually, with elegant casual black trousers on delicate blue and red stripes. He was wearing a silk shirt in dark and light green, and on top of it – a sleeveless jumper. He was sweaty all over and burning with desire to see me die in agony. I could feel him shaking. He was a cousin of one of the bodyguards I had killed. I could hear his teeth clenching. He was transmitting waves of furious hatred.

There was a woman next to him, about 35 years old. She had an elegant blue silk suit. The top part consisted of a backless strapped bodice. The bottom part was a short pleated skirt. She also had a transparent shirt with long pleated around the wrists sleeves. She looked like a naughty school-girl who just discovered what masturbation was about and nothing else mattered at that moment. She was showing signs of strong sexual arousal. She was twisting her arms backwards, quite involuntarily, and was squeezing them together. She was breathing heavily. What she really wanted to know at that moment was whether I had an erection. That woman was the district attorney, assigned to my case.

Then there was another sweet creature with glasses and such a slash on the side of the skirt that I could see the edge of her red panties. She was wearing a slightly suggestive dress. She looked like a maid, just heading out of the master's bedroom, having finished her bedroom duties. That woman was a writer of detective stories. Her black sparkling eyes wanted to soak up everything that was going on around me. She wanted to put me in her next novel. She was all adrenaline and genuine interest.

Next to her there was an important-looking gentleman in a formal black suit, dark blue silk shirt and a black tie. He wasn't clean-shaven; it was more like he had a three-day beard on. He was pouring out some wild animal cruelty and a strong desire to see me squirm from the electric shock! He was also showing his disappointment from my pardoning. He was the chief of police in that city. I could "see" his thoughts for a moment – he was imagining how he was firing at everybody present, and then letting the electric shock kill me, while in the same time I was begging him for mercy and screaming in terror... Hmmm... Maybe a psychiatrist could help there?

Then it was the prison chief's turn. He was dressed in clothes, more appropriate for someone who's going to get executed – grey and nondescript. He was grey and nondescript himself. Hair, prematurely turned grey and silver, showing no emotions whatsoever, just mere boredom of having to sit here instead of drinking himself to sleep with cheap whiskey, for instance.

Next I could see a man with his mouth gapped and saliva stringing from its left corner. He was wearing an extremely fashionable elegant suit with an impressive large collar and a white shirt with the same striking collar, placed onto the suit's collar. He was holding an elegant top hat in his hands, and his white gloves were placed in it. As part of the stage-setting he was carrying a romantic-looking cane. He was showing… mmm…. A passionate desire to hold me close and …. Oh, well, he was the chief of police's lover.

Then there was this tough-looking fifty-something lady, dressed in a formal old-fashioned black dress. She was wearing an enormous hat. She had an old lorgnette in front of her eyes. At present she resented the fact that I was still alive, that is, that Evil went unpunished! She was the chairperson of the Pious Society. I've never heard of it before, but an inner voice told me those people were church regulars and were praying for the extinction of anything evil. They also issued a weekly newspaper and a daily TV show. All in all, these were their public activities.

And last, but not least, there was an ordinary-looking woman in her thirties. Casual clothes – jeans and a denim jacket. Long fluffy black hair. Black eyes. She was radiating Pure Joy and smiling. She was a friend of the girl the cops shot right before my eyes and thus, getting their punishment. She was clutching her hands tightly, as if she was praying that lucky turn of fate was true. I couldn't control myself, I smiled at her and she jumped from her seat.

For a moment I though I was going crazy...

Then the vision was gone.

I was dazzled.

What the hell was that? Did I actually see it or ...?

I got up from the chair and stretched out until my bones cracked. I pushed back my wet hair (because of the electrolyte liquid in the sponge).

I nodded to those behind the mirror and to the armed guards.

It felt like I wasn't all there in the room. As if I had my foot in the afterlife, so to say.

I looked at Elizabeth. I was waiting for instructions. She held me by the arm and led me ahead. I was watching the way distractedly. My brain was still thinking about the vision in the room.

No, it couldn't have been my imagination. I really did see the people behind the mirror. I saw them quite clearly, with every detail. I even ... sensed them from afar. I knew what each of them was thinking and feeling.

Basically, I know that things like that are possible and some experience them on a regular basis. It's just that I didn't expect this to happen to me.

Could I possibly make it happen again, this time deliberately, with the sheer power of my will… whenever I feel like it?

Elizabeth took me to my cell to collect my things. They weren't that much.

None of the guards and wardens accompanied us.

I was now pardoned.

I was also property of Elizabeth's masters.

I didn't care very much about it at that moment. It really wasn't that big of a deal. I was only interested in my recent vision. There had to be a reason for it to happen. Some people develop these abilities after near-death experiences. Was that the case with me? Well, I didn't really have one of those, or did I?

Along the corridors, along the corridors, then inside the inner yard, pass like ten inner gates and barbed wire electric fences, all the way to the main gate.

Near the gate a dark-blue serious-looking van was parked. A robust brute in a dark blue suit was standing next to it. He looked condescendingly at me from top to bottom and opened the side sliding door for me. I got in. The door slid behind me. Elizabeth remained outside. Obviously, her part was to be played elsewhere. The windows of the van were darkened from the outside. There were two folding benches on the two sides. There were two more beasts in suits on each of them. One of the brutes greeted me with a nod and said dryly:

"Give me your hands to put the handcuffs on."

I hummed and followed the order. They put a bag on my head. I couldn't see a thing.

It didn't feel like pardoning to me.

It felt like I was bent forward, and there was this Huge One, greased with Vaseline, behind me.

Yeah, as if shit had never happened to me before!

Actually, since I have this bag on anyway, why don't I think about it a little?

First, I was furious about the execution fiasco and the eleventh-hour pardoning. To hell with them! Why couldn't they pardon me a little bit earlier? I was already preparing for my journey "to the other side". But, no, sir! They took that away from me. They wanted to extract the maximum pleasure of giving my life back when they felt like it. They are playing God with me, damn it! And who knows with how many people more! And they expect gratitude or, more likely, they think I owe them something. Just because they decided to let me live on a whim! Not out of the goodness of their hearts, but because they can squeeze a little bit more out of me.

Is the mouse grateful when the cat releases it on a whim? No! The mouse wants to become a lion and tear the cat's butt in pieces! Well, that's what I wanted now!

Secondly, why did they pick *me*? I was so insignificant, I didn't mean a thing. Why me? What job could I possibly do for them? What were they planning to use me for?

No, that's useless. Let's look at things from a different angle.

Some time ago, when I wacked that congressman, I never got the death penalty. Who was interested to poke things around and sentence me to death? Were the sentence and the pardon secured yesterday? In the same time? Isn't that just a show to scare me off and for them to feel great and to know they could do whatever they want when it comes to justice and power?

I started listening to what was going on around me.

I smelled the mawkish perfumes of the two bodyguards. I could hear their heavy breathing. Maybe they both were overweight. The one kept coughing. Smoking too much, my friend? The other kept stretching and crackling his joints. He must be a heavy-lifter who messed up his cartilages. The driver was changing gears rather stiffly. The van hummed, jumped and coughed.

The two guys inside didn't say a word to each other.

The van was doing 60. I could hear the cars outside. I listened to the various city noises. Now and then, somebody honked. A police car passed by, followed by an ambulance. In any case, the City was buzzing without a care in this world, without caring about us in the van, unless I broke the rules in some way. Then it usually sends its forces to put us neatly back in the box.

So why should I care about the City?

We left the city. Apparently, we were driving on the highway, because we were speeding up. Faster and faster… the speed limit was 140, I think. I guess that was our speed at the moment.

Where were we going?

Did some relatives of the people I killed want me for themselves?

Was I supposed to kill somebody?

We drove about 40 – 45min on the highway, then we took an exit. We passed a small town. Once more I heard the familiar city noises of car engines, horns and things like that, but less than the one in the Big City. We left the small town, too. At a certain point we turned to a third-class road. Another half an hour or so passed. Finally, we turned to a dirt road. The van was jumping on some lumps and stones.

I didn't have the slightest idea where we were going.

The car stopped and I heard a dog barking.

Was that a mansion of some sorts?

An iron gate opened – I could hear a slight screeching of metal pressing metal. The van moved forward a few feet and stopped. I guess we parked in the yard. The gate closed behind us. The engine went dead.

One of the bodyguards stood up, his joints cracked again, slid the side door and got off. Dogs ran to the van – I heard their lolling breath and I could smell them. They came to meet the guest.

I heard birds singing.

The other brute coughed a little, moved around and took off the bag.

I blinked instinctively. I didn't need to, it was night-time.

The dogs were staring at me right next to the van. Rottweilers, pretty strong animals.

I stood up and also stretched as far as I could in the handcuffs. The dogs snarled quietly.

Outside, the bodyguard shushed them in a familiar way and chased them away from the van. I got off in the yard. It was quite large, surrounded by a high stone wall and solid metal gate. A large two-storey house of hewn stone blocks stood in the back.

I was able to see all that because of the few big spotlights installed on the wall and the house. I also saw security cameras.

That was a genuine fortress.

One of the brutes in suits (obviously dying for a fag) lit a cigarette and inhaled fiercely.

The other cracked his neck, came to me and smiled patronizingly:

"Move it!"

I shrugged, "Where to?"

He reached, grabbed me on the neck and slightly squeezing, repeated:

"Move it!"

"Where to?" I persisted.

He squeezed me really tight this time.

"Move it, you little piece of shit!"

I knew that if I didn't do anything quickly, I'd pass out.

I knelt abruptly, twisted my body in his direction and stood up at once. I bent his arm in the elbow, as if he wanted to rest it on his waist. I lifted his arm up and his grasp loosened. If he had caught me in time, he could have grabbed me on the lower part of the neck. But I was quick and sharp. He let go. I kicked him in the knee with the same abrupt manner. The joint cracked and he knelt with a deep sigh. With my other foot I gave him a vicious kick in the chin from below. He twisted his head, fell on his back and fell silent.

That was a minor problem.

All of a sudden, the two Rottweilers decided to eat me for breakfast. As I already mentioned, they were bulky and ferocious.

The second bodyguard put the cigarette out and shouted them to lie down, but the adrenaline had overwhelmed them.

They were about ten feet away, but now were heading straight in my direction. One of them was faster. That was okay with me; I prefer one on one combats.

When it came a feet or so away, the large dog jumped vigorously at my chest. Obviously, that was how they had trained it to pull out the intruders' teeth. Good boy! I stepped ever so slightly aside and when he drew level with me I kicked him in the throat with the tip of my shoe. It fell down squeaking in convulsions.

If it had been a smart dog, the second one would have given up, or at least would have shown a more untraditional approach. Well, it wasn't a smart dog. It repeated the same trick. I repeated my trick. Unfortunately, I missed its throat and kicked him in the stomach. It fell down badly, with a cough. It looked at me in panic.

I came near:

"Now you'll beg, didn't you want to bite me by the throat just a second ago?"

I kicked it in the ribs five or six times. It started whining in-between the cough and the breathing attempts.

Iron cracked. I turned round. The second bodyguard was aiming a gun at me. He looked resolute.

I shrugged, "Just tell me which way to go."

He nodded and put away the piece. He pointed, "To the house."

Chapter 6

turned around and headed for the house. See how easy-going I am?

I didn't notice before, but there were five more brutes with guns near the gate. Cordial welcome, isn't it? Gallant hosts. The men looked vicious and were ready to shoot. When I leveled with them, one of them hissed:

"These are good dogs, you stupid shit! They were just going to knock you down without hurting you. If you messed them up, I'd kick the shit out of you!"

I stopped and glanced at him:

"I don't know anything about dogs. And I don't have good manners. Is there anything else?"

He clutched his jaws and shriveled a little. I was preparing myself to kick his ass. The bodyguard, accompanying me to the house, swiftly moved between us, grabbed me by the left shoulder and slightly pushed me:

"Let's go inside."

I climbed four steps and entered the house. The front door was solid wood with metal plates. The house itself, as you probably remember, was made of solid stone blocks. The corridor inside was all marble. There were some animal furs spread on the floor. Large pictures were hanging from the walls. Apparently, the owners were into grandeur. They were probably living in a small world of their own with knights and princesses. Enormous chandeliers were hanging from the ceiling.

It was a short corridor, leading to a vast antechamber. Actually, it was a huge antechamber turned into a living-room. It was about ten by ten. On the opposite side of the room, a large stone staircase was leading to the second floor.

There were doors on both sides of the staircase. Obviously, the antechamber was surrounded by a corridor behind the walls, outflanking the whole first floor. There were two more doors on the two side walls, most likely leading to the corridor as well. The second floor probably had a similar architectural design. Maybe the basement floor, too. It must have had a basement floor, no doubt about it.

In the living-room/antechamber there were ten or so sofas lined up along the walls. There were a few solid wood tables. A medium-sized bookcase was placed near the right wall. It was meant to impress visitors, suggesting that the owners are intelligent people.

There was a large fire-place on the left. And in front of it – a big sofa and three comfy armchairs. An elderly white-haired gentleman in a thick vest rose from one of the armchairs. If he hadn't stood up, I wouldn't have seen him, because both the sofa and the armchairs had high backs, and weren't facing the antechamber. So that whoever was sitting, could watch the flames in the fireplace.

The man stepped forward. He had well-kept beard and moustaches, also white. He was holding a book, marking the page he was reading with his left index finger.

Dark brown eyes. Fixing gaze. Obviously, that was the owner.

He looked at me inquisitively for about a minute, then let a condescending smile and said with a soft deep voice:

"Take the handcuffs off."

The bodyguard hesitated and chipped in:

"Are you sure? 'Cos he just…"

The man waved, "Take them off!"

His voice was incredibly powerful. The guard obeyed at once, just like a puppet on a string. The host invited me to sit down on the sofa in front of the fireplace with a broad aristocratic gesture.

I came nearer. He stretched his hand:

"Alistair Conroy the Twelfth, pleased to meet you."

I took his hand and shook it cordially, "Sevar Godrack, the first and only, pleased to meet you, too!"

He smiled faintly at my fanfaronade and pointed at the sofa. We sat next to each other. He was at my right. He put his book aside and smiled at me.

"You're always trying to impress, aren't you?"

"What do you mean?' I lifted an eyebrow.

"What did you do in the yard?"

"I was given a cordial welcome," I shrugged, "so I responded the same way."

He looked at the bodyguard, standing behind me. He immediately reported subserviently:

"He battered Mac and the two rottweilers."

My host smiled again. The bodyguard added in the same subservient manner:

"With his hands handcuffed in the back."

The host's eyebrows went so far above, I thought he'd lose them. He nodded thoughtfully. Then smiled again. At this point, I wanted to throw this smile through the door. I might not even open the door first. That smile was fake and meticulously worked on. I don't like hypocrites!

"You really know how to impress people!" he said with a carefully measured dose of admiration.

"Thank you," I nodded, "and you know how to work people very well."

I could see in his gaze some discontent, surprise and … just a touch of cruelty. Now I got him, that son of a bitch, he wanted to be in control and dominate, and if anybody disobeyed him, he got furious. A megalomaniac. A sick mind.

Aren't we all?

"I think I owe you an explanation as of why I invited you here." he said solemnly.

Invited, huh?

I nodded in silence.

"Would you like something to drink?"

I looked at the big clock on the right of the fireplace. It was 4 o'clock; definitely not the time for alcohol.

"May I have a triple coffee?" I asked.

He reached and grabbed a small bell from the table near the sofa. He rang three times. A black maid in a formal, military-like uniform and a strange bonnet appeared out of nowhere. She just flew in from the door on the left of the fireplace and the clock. She halted in front of us in quiet expectation.

I have to admit she was slim and beautiful, and besides, I'm not fastidious.

"The gentleman would like a triple coffee," ordered the host, "I'll take a cup of green tea!"

The woman flew away.

"Blacks always serve better than whites." Alistair Conroy shared with me, "they're more obedient and are not pretentious."

I nodded understandingly.

"By the way, what are your views on race and gender?" he wanted to know.

"Well…", I stuttered, "The Negroes are black, because the sun is too strong there, while the Asians live in very windy conditions and keep squinting at the wind, that's why their eyes are slanted…"

He laughed whole-heartily. For a brief moment he almost looked like a good and candid man. The beverages arrived on a table with wheels. There was also a gilt porcelain sugar-bowl and a plate with pastry. My coffee was poured in a low wide thick-stemmed cup, and the tea – in a tall exquisite cup, gilt on the edge. There were two jugs – for milk and cream. I wanted to thank the maid, but all I managed to see was her left heel, vanishing behind the door. That's right; there were all kinds of professional behavior.

The host put two lumps of sugar in his cup, poured some milk, and by doing so, totally fucked up his tea, stirred it and gracefully sipped with pleasure. Obviously, he was into rituals. I was curious if he had a wife, children, relatives? Who could stand such a person? If his bed manners were the same, he probably proceeded only with the co-operation of professional ladies of pleasure, or he was gay.

I put three lumps of sugar, stirred my coffee hard and tried it. It was tasty and strong.

"How's your coffee?" my host seemed intrigued.

"I like it."

"This is an extremely rare sort of Nicaraguan coffee," his eyes were sparkling, "it has no name. It is exhaustingly hard to import it; it is very expensive and appreciated by true connoisseurs! Can you feel the thick luscious flavor?" He was looking at me, almost in a state of trance.

"The coffee is really good," I nodded, "I like it. But to be honest, I can't tell even the most common brands, unless it's something extremely disgusting. I know nothing about coffee."

He became slightly dejected. I couldn't appreciate the flavor, the style and the grandeur. He decided he had just cast pearls before the swine, obviously. Well, get over it, pal, life's not fair.

"It is time to announce why you are here," he swallowed the insult and his disappointment in me, "as you have probably guessed, I repealed your death sentence. I have friends, partners and debtors in high places." He smiled indulgently.

"I thought so," I nodded, "probably it was you, who secured that sentence in the first place."

His tea suddenly felt bitter. He looked at me with discontent:

"You guess too much. Apparently, you're not as dumb, as the reports say."

"I'm sorry," I shrugged, "I can try harder. I'm a diligent student, really."

He looked even more displeased, and then nodded. Obviously, I was a hard nut to crack. He smiled faintly and decided to play. Surely, he wanted me badly, so he was going to be patient.

Why, the hell, would he need me?

"I'm the brother of the congressman you killed some time ago, Godrack."

He looked at me straight in the eyes, waiting for my reaction. There wasn't any.

"You don't seem surprised." He noted the fact.

"I guessed you might be a relative of one of those bastards." I said coldly and now he was surprised. "I don't regret killing them and I don't feel sorry for any of them! If I could turn back time, I would kill them all again! I'm sorry for only one thing – I couldn't crush them before they murdered the girl!"

Then I took a sip of my coffee. It was really good. My complements to the black maid!

It seemed Alistair Conroy had forgotten about his tea. He was standing with his mouth open, staring blankly at me. A drop of cream was slowly making its way through his beard and below. I felt the urge to reach and wipe it fatherly … on the fireplace's sharp edge.

At last he spoke quietly, "You are in my home. I let you drink my coffee and sit with me on the same sofa. Few have received such honor. I don't think you appreciate it enough. I may reconsider my attitude towards you. You've seen just a few of my dogs outside. Please, don't miscalculate the situation. I could kill you right now and the only thing you could do about it is watch it happen. Don't confuse my good will with weakness!"

I stared at him for about a minute. I was wondering if I could reach out, break his neck right away, then take the fireplace tongs and kill his … dogs, and after that call the black maid and finish my coffee while she was reading me extracts of that book…

I decided to wait a while longer.

So I smiled and said:

"I was being rude. I apologize for abusing your hospitality. I meant no offence."

As if with a magic wand he brightened up. He smiled (sincerely, this time) and announced generously:

"Never mind, I forgive you. I can see you do not hold dear the memory of my brother. Your reaction is understandable. I am not angry with you."

He took a sip from his tea. With the corner of my eye I could see the bodyguard putting away the gun in the holster under his left armpit.

"Truth be told, I must say I do not cherish good memories of my brother as well," announced solemnly Alistair Conroy, XII "putting aside that he was my half-brother, a product of my mother's minor affair, he was a total rascal. He didn't appreciate the things he had. I gave him unlimited opportunities. He was spending all of his time in meaningless animal amusement! Yes, he was a brainless, narrow-minded asshole!"

I was looking at him thoughtfully. I think he meant everything he said.

"Actually, the only smart thing my brother ever did," the host went on after a sip of tea, "was to happen to be near you. That way you relieved me of the obligation to take care of that dumb creature and gave me the opportunity to get acquainted with you. I have to give him that!" he smiled.

He was definitely mad. He looked upon people, as if he were a king, and they were pawns, knights, rooks... but mainly pawns.

"I'll tell you a story," he looked askance at me.

"I love a good story," I smiled, "especially a scary one."

"Don't worry, it's scary enough." he nodded seriously.

I got ready to listen.

"Once upon a time, there was a father and his three sons." he started. "The father was very clever. Besides being a very good and wealthy merchant, which secured his sons' lives, he was also very good at natural sciences. He has discovered the electricity in the dawn of the human history. His knowledge was vast and he had some incredible achievements in the sphere of the occult."

He drank some tea for the necessary dramatic pause.

"Once, a very strange guest arrived at their house. He offered the father an even stranger deal," he looked at me to see if I was intrigued enough. "Can you guess what kind of a deal?"

I shook my head and sipped some coffee.

"He claimed he was a messenger of the Creator of the World. He explained the Creator was tired of its creation and now wanted to delegate the responsibility to somebody else. That was an angel. The Creator had recognized the father's powerful mind, multi-skills and sense of responsibility. He offered the father and his sons to take care of this World, and in exchange he would bless them with Immortality and iron constitution. The father thought about it for three days and finally accepted the Divine Responsibility. On his leaving, the angel left him this huge book with all the World's secrets. He didn't mention there was somebody else, also interested in this World. The Creator's archrival. That enemy wanted to conquer the World and bring it under his evil sway. The rival came after a couple of days and also presented an offer – the father would grant him the ruling of the World and the rival would spare his sons' lives, as well as his own. Naturally, the father refused. (What's natural about it, I have no idea). Satan left very annoyed and sent his army of demons on the very same day. It was a great battle. A monstrous storm was destroying the whole area, miles and miles around, stones with the size of houses were flying, thunderbolts were tearing the sky, hundred-year old trees were falling down, split in halves. Many people though that was the End of the World. In the end, you could hear only the cries of the dying demons and monsters; their blood, black as coal, was covering the earth for miles around. The father and his sons defeated the army from hell. But they had to go deep underground. Nobody remembers them now. Only a few know this story. It is completely forgotten." He smiled, "Well, a few still remember. The four lead sometimes hidden and sometimes open war against Satan for thousands of years. That war goes on till this very day."

I was sipping my coffee. That was a really good story, though I doubted it was true. But the coffee was excellent! Where did that black maid go? She was excellent, too!

"You don't believe a word I say, do you?" my host asked me, "I don't mind. Nobody would believe it until they see it with their own eyes."

"Even if I believed you, that is of no concern of mine. I don't give a damn about the father and his sons, or Satan, or the people and this World."

He laughed:

"I expected that. It is said in your evaluation paper, 'Dangerously careless regarding his own existence, as well as that of others, which could lead to sudden bursts of violence and aggression.' Okay… but if Satan gets you, I assure you, you'll quickly change your tune."

"It's possible." I sipped some coffee.

"It seems impossible to you to feel fear or pain, but if that happens, you'll wish you were invisible, or never been born; you'll definitely wish you had powerful friends."

"It's possible," I sipped some more coffee.

"My offer is for you to join us. Join our Society, my army. Become part of us. By doing so, your meaningless intake of breath, water, food and excretion you call life at the moment, will acquire purpose and meaning. And, who knows, you may even feel happiness."

He was looking at me expectantly. I sipped some more.

"What do you think?" he asked impatiently.

I hummed. I finished my coffee and put down the cup in the saucer on the table.

"Truth be told," I started, "I thought you wanted me to kill somebody. It's fair and square, and I could understand that. Then I thought you wanted to kill me with your own hands as revenge for your brother's death. This is also fair and square and I could understand it, too." I helped myself with a cookie. "But you're telling me such vague and opaque stories. I don't understand them. You want me to join your army and fight Satan, to protect people? Honestly, I never really liked people. I consider them to be extremely wicked! I've never been interested in people, except the ones close to me. You say the Creator got tired of its creation? In my opinion, he didn't want to admit he had made such a Lousy and Wicked World; that he had made a really big mistake. It would have been gallant for him to admit it. You say, Satan wants to conquer the World and enslave us? Same difference, I say!"

"Darkness will fall upon us, oppression, unseen perversions; lawlessness, violence, disease and death are awaiting us! Demons will dominate over people, use and abuse them in any way they want! The World will suffer in darkness and despair!" he looked exalted, eyes wide open, fanatic sparkle and determination in his eyes.

"I don't see the difference," I said with cold indifference and took a bite from the cookie.

He was surprised, astonished even! He was speechless.

I finished my cookie and asked:

"Tell me, however, if I decided to join you, what would my part be? And all in all, your nice story needs proof. Who is the father? Who are his sons? Tell me more about them. Give me some historical data."

"I'll give you some data," he nodded, "I can see you are a man of logic and thinking. Let's discuss, for example, the dictators that really made their mark – Attila, Genghis Khan, Alexander the Great, Napoleon… they all rose to power with the help of the father and his sons."

"Is that really true?" I was curious.

"Yes, it's true," he nodded, "but for your peace of mind, I'll tell you that you are about to find out for yourself really soon, when you see the indisputable facts."

"I can hardly wait."

He nodded and drank some tea. I was quite intrigued, actually. I wanted to see the evidence.

"Let me finish," he started again, "as I said, the father was a clever man. He knew if he was to fight Satan, he had to win the people on his side. People can be easily sold and bought, alas for a short time! You can win them for the longest time possible through religion. He created the Ten Commandments, just for starters. In that way he was able to unite some of the people by making them believe in an idea, though it wasn't the True one. People need constant persuasion and proof, though. And in the same time he had to lead a war against Satan and its legions of demons. The two elder brothers took up the people. For centuries they persuaded people to mind their own business and thus, not be influenced by Satan. On the youngest brother's shoulders, who was the most experienced in the Secret Sciences, fell the grave responsibility to lead the hidden war against Satan and its demons."

He rang three times with the bell. The black cutie showed up by the sofa.

"Bring us some breakfast." ordered the host.

I looked at the clock on the wall. It was ten to five. It was time for a snack, indeed. In a minute it was here – big plates, well laden with various kinds of meat, cheese and fruit, and toasted bread. And more tea and coffee. That maid is really something!

I poured myself more coffee. The host started spreading butter on a piece of toast and continued his story:

"The two brothers initially created Judaism as a unifying religion. Then decided to develop it farther into Christianity. The perfect example of self-sacrifice for the Common Good, hoping people would take up the idea and prepare to die for one another."

"That didn't work, right?" I asked skeptically.

"Unfortunately, it didn't." he sighed. "The two brothers decided to change strategy. They knew well that people unite against a common enemy. Only then they are completely unanimous. That's why they created the other religions. They opposed people from different religions, and united people who shared the same religions. And that is how they successfully accomplished their primary goal – to distract people's attention from the Archenemy – Satan. That is not its real name, though."

"They mention It in all religions, I think." I put in.

"Not all," he shook his head, "and besides, it is always depicted in such a way as to distract the readers' attention from the Real True Satan. You see," he looked at me gravely, "most of the time they say that Satan convinces people it didn't exist. So that it could work in secret. The truth, however, is exactly the other way round. It never intended to hide. It was the one who almost never lied. But people don't pay It any attention, because their attention is constantly distracted."

"By the three brothers, you mean?"

"By the two brothers. The third one is leading the war against It."

"How could It be here from the Very Beginning of Things and nobody could see It?" I was amazed. "And why don't the two brothers just show It to us and say, Here It is! Crush It completely!'"

He smiled patronizingly and shook his head:

"It is neither ugly nor frightening. There is no man on this earth, who could see It and not succumb to Its beauty, Its glory and Its charm. There is no man who could see It and not follow it."

He put down his toast.

"As far as us not seeing It... We can't see the electricity, either, but it could shake us really hard and kill us in seconds. We can't see the magnetic field, either but it could drive us insane. Do you need more?"

"No," I shook my head, "you convinced me. I have one question, though."

"What is it?"

"Are you a direct descendant of any of the three brothers?"

He smiled happily:

"I am a direct descendent of the eldest brother's bloodline! My forefathers have been making the World's History for centuries! Now this task is mine."

He smiled happily again.

"And what exactly did your ancestors do?"

"As I said, they understood that, unfortunately, people only unite against a common enemy. In reality, my forefathers were responsible for any major armed conflict and for any major social change in general! Of course, they couldn't do it on their own. That's why they set an orderly organization which led societies and peoples through the centuries."

"Masonry?" I asked, "Knights Templar?"

"The Knights Templar belong to the youngest brother," he retorted, "they directly fight Satan's followers. Masons, yes. Sometimes it's them, sometimes – others. Whatever and whoever is necessary."

I gave him one more patronizing smile. The guy was really crazy.

Usually, people like him make me extremely furious. These guys, playing God, insist on dominating over others in an open and uncompromising way. They drive me mad.

"So, what you're trying to say," I took another cookie "is that you're proud with your family for making people kill each other? Let me ask you this, why don't you leave it all to Satan? It will finish the job much quicker and with better quality."

He flustered with anger. Shaking with fury and hissing with indignation, he said in a mean trembling voice:

"You are an arrogant, irresponsible, selfish and narrow-minded idiot!"

I nodded in agreement.

"Isn't there anything in this world that interests you?"

"There probably is," I replied coldly, "and some day I may find it."

"You're totally insane!" his hands were shaking, "I'm starting to regret sparing your life!"

"Actually," I ate the last crumble of my cookie, "there is one thing that interests me at the moment." I looked him intently.

He stared at me.

"And that is," I continued, "how come a nobody like you thinks he's better than anyone else? Do you think you'd like this "Playing God" game, if someone else was playing God on you?"

Chapter 7

"No one knows what he is capable of until he tries.

Publius Syrus

He opened his eyes wide and was about to say something but I had already grabbed the sugar-bowl and with a slight twist I threw it in the face of the bodyguard behind me. He quickly ducked to avoid it and lost me from his sight. I jumped over the back of the sofa, and when he finally stood up, I was in his face. He goggled and opened his mouth in the same moment when my forehead was crushing his nose. He lost his strength. I grabbed him by the collar and tossed him around, acting as my shield against Alistair Conroy, XII. Just in case. It turned out I was right – Conroy took out a gun and started shooting and screaming incoherently. His pride and dignity followed his heart straight into his heels.

I knew that in a second all the mansion watchdogs would gather in the strange antechamber. I had no time to lose!

I threw the guard's body on the sofa and jumped on the left to the table with the food and cutlery. Conroy drew a bead on me right before I kicked the small table in his direction. If he were a professional killer, he would have fired at me before I kicked that table. Then he would have backed out gracefully on the side and filled my body with bullets. But he wasn't a pro. He instinctively protected himself by reaching out his hands. Instincts can be a bitch sometimes! A moment after the table hit him in the legs, I was right beside him. I got hold of the gun with my right hand, and with my left I grabbed his hair. I took the gun away, and grabbed him even harder. The hair remained where it belonged… for now. I grabbed the back of his neck, fixing his throat between my biceps and the armpit of my left arm. Then I grabbed the right side of my collar. With a single strong squeeze I paralyzed him. If I kept doing that for ten lousy seconds, someone else would get promoted instead of him.

In that moment, four armed men barged in. They were probably the same men I saw by the staircase. It was about time! I was beginning to worry about them! I was starting to miss them.

The minute they saw I was holding their boss in such an uncomfortable position, they halted with guns pointing at me.

"He's a Devil's servant!" Conroy shouted all of a sudden, "His soul is long lost! Kill him!"

"That's a bad decision!" I growled, "If I go, you go with me!"

The men hesitated. Good. I had to crush them quickly, before they decided to act on it.

"Here's what I suggest," I started, "I'm taking your boss hostage. You let me go in peace, and I gratefully let him go afterwards."

They exchanged glances. Alistair Conroy the Twelfth was about to say something. I politely pushed his throat to prevent him from ruining the good impression my speech had. The brutes (already amounting to ten, all armed) cast a glance at one another. Then one of them nodded, lowered his gun and said:

"It's a deal."

So, you're the alpha dog, I'll remember that just in case.

Everybody lowered their guns. Holding Alistair Conroy, XII lovingly from behind, I delicately left the scene, avoiding the shooters. The two of us went out in the yard. I could see a couple of things. First, I saw the van they brought me in. Then the two dogs and the bodyguard I 'danced with' when we arrived. The rottweilers didn't want to kiss and make up. The guard looked mean at me and reached for his holster.

"FYI," I cut short his enthusiasm, "Mister Conroy and I are going on a honeymoon, and you'll stay here to watch over the house."

He still wanted to play; I could see it in his eyes.

"When we satisfy our lust for each other," I added, "I'm letting your boss go safe and sound. You have my word!"

His face straightened and he let go of the holster. I nodded. We reached the van. I said to Conroy:

"We have a little problem. We both have to get in the van. But you want to run away and I don't want to let you go just yet. What do you think? Do you think we could both get in without me hurting you?"

He thought for a while, and then said:

"All right. I won't try to run."

"Ok, I believe you."

I opened the driver's door. With the corner of my eye I could see that the brutes were crowding the yard.

"Get in." I said to Conroy, releasing my deathly grip.

He sat behind the wheel. I stepped on the footboard:

"Move to the passenger's seat!"

I could see the anger and the disappointment in his eyes, but he moved anyway. I sat in the driver's seat and closed the door. The key was in the ignition. I started the engine.

"Put your seatbelt on," I said to Conroy, "anything could happen. There are reckless drivers everywhere, and I am an easily-scared, bad driver."

He buckled up really angry. Now he had one more obstacle, in case he decided to run away. I reached out and locked his door, just to be on the safe side.

"How are you planning to get out?" he asked, "The gate is armored."

"Put your window down and tell them to open it." I answered coldly.

"And why would I do that?" he exclaimed sarcastically.

"Oh, you *don't have to* do it," I glanced at him, "Do it only if you want to live."

His hesitation lasted exactly two seconds. Then he put down his window and shouted to open the gate. Here we were, leaving the fortress at last.

"Now what?" Conroy asked.

"Now you'll tell me two things; first, what is the assignment you had planned for me?"

"And the second?"

"Let's take it slow. Tell me what the assignment is."

He fell silent. Maybe he was hesitating. I didn't have the patience for that.

"Please," I growled, "tell me."

"Do you remember the three gentlemen who visited you in prison the other day?" he asked.

I nodded, "Yes."

"They are working on a secret project."

"Sure. So what?"

"This project concerns the creation of a super warrior."

I shook my head. As long as there are people living in this World, it will never get better!

"C'mon! Why don't they try something new and different for once?" I murmured with discontent.

"You were one of the potential candidates." Conroy went on.

"No, I'm not." I replied.

"You are cunning, skilful, quick and strong-minded," he continued, "furthermore, you are cold and callous. No touchy-feely emotions stand in your way. You have no scruples. You are the perfect candidate!"

I shook my head and stared at him, "You have no idea how wrong you are!"

I sighed:

"You're taking me to meet your buddies."

"Impossible! They are part of a Secret Organization!"

"I know," I nodded, "Take me to them."

"I can't! If we go, they'll kill us!"

"Excellent! What a perfect opportunity to see if I really *am* the perfect candidate!" I smiled dryly.

He looked at me in a mixture of astonishment, admiration and total lack of understanding.

"You really *are* the One!"

"I am the perfect candidate," I replied coldly, "to become your enemy. There are two ways about it. You take me of your own free will. Or you take me after I convince you to. And I guarantee you, I will convince you."

"You'll have to kill me first!" he said with unexpected harshness.

I looked at him disapprovingly for about ten seconds. It took me two minutes to think it over.

The van surely had GPS and they were monitoring our every move. They knew exactly where we were. Probably two vans with brutes were driving at a close distance. As long as Conroy stayed in the van, nothing bad was going to happen. They just couldn't be sure that I won't hurt him. But, if we stopped, they would surely catch us.

Should I let them catch me? They will probably do a whole bunch of unpleasant things to me. They had to get back at me for my performance back there.

"We can go to the Sheraton Hotel," I suggested "we could register as a newlywed couple with our real names."

He was astonished.

"I think you don't have the guts to die," I nodded at him "you want to live a while longer and play God. I think you are really afraid of dying."

He goggled.

"Actually," I continued to contemplate. "What do I need you for in the first place?"

There was horror in his gaze, just like a homosexual who has just been outed in public.

I said, "You'd better open that door and jump out while we're still moving, I don't have to drag you with me anymore."

We were driving on a dirt road with approximately 50 mph. I wasn't familiar with the road and the area.

"You can't just throw me out while we are still moving!" he exclaimed, "I'll kill myself!"

"Why can't I?" I was surprised "You can pick me for one of your soldiers; you can sentence me to death and then pardon me! I only want to kill you and you're being fussy! Shame on you!"

He was amazed; he was sitting with his mouth open.

"Call your guys; tell them I agreed to become your soldier."

He wasn't astonished any more. He was dumbfounded. His eyes were open wide. He wanted to say something, but was only able to produce a couple of inarticulate sounds.

"Tell them you convinced me somehow." I went on with my suggestions. "You had explained your master plan and I was amazed, enthralled and overcome by it! I cried, I begged you on my knees to be enlisted!"

He kept opening and closing his mouth. I think its hinges were squeaking.

I added, "Tell them you stroke my ego, telling me what a wonderful, lovely superhero I was! You bedazzled me, brainwashed me, and turned me upside down! Tell them you made me a new man! A moving zombie," I winked and grinned "I begged you with tears in my eyes to take me with you. I even gave you a blowjob, just to let you know how devoted I was to you!"

"You're insane" he stuttered in terror.

"People tell me that all the time." I replied gloomily.

He continued, "People tend to avoid danger, and you are searching for it. I don't get you…"

"I am no "people"" I hissed "Now, call your men, gather them up and take me there."

He was silent for a couple of minutes. I was driving without saying a word. I knew that Alistair Conroy the Twelfth had already decided to take me to his people. Everything was about to clear up. That is precisely how I like it – all above-board. Everything on the surface. No beating about the bush.

"May I call on my cell?" Conroy asked.

"Sure."

I didn't listen to who and what he was talking about; his conversation was no concern of mine.

I was planning what I was going to do when I see all those sons of bitches gathered in one place. They would probably expect me. They would probably be prepared. They would probably be armed to the teeth. They would probably want to kill me.

Then what?

I was left with only one thing.

I had to kill them all.

For one brief moment, the World would be able to take a deep breath of fresh untainted air.

And as for me…

I'll see to that after I'm done with them.

Conroy finished his phone call and looked at me:

"It's done."

"Where are they?"

"In a small hotel, 'The Heart of the City.'"

"I know where it is." I replied, "How many people will be there, you think?"

"I don't know," he was honest about it "may be five, maybe ten, maybe the whole hotel and the block will be crowded with soldiers."

"Excellent!" I grinned happily "The more, the merrier!"

He was sending me mixed signals again. He shook his head:

"Really, you're sick! How I wish you were playing for our team! Truly!"

"You don't want that, believe me." I answered seriously.

"I do!"

"You are looking for heartless and brainless soldiers, and I am none of the above!" I explained.

"Yeah, right!" he snapped "So sensitive you are! Every time I think about how you killed the congressman with the back of the gun... how you taught those prisoners a lesson... You are all Mercy and Compassion!"

"I'm not talking about mercy here." I replied coldly "Do you think I would kill that shit with the back of a gun if I were cold and heartless?"

I looked at him inquisitively. He would still not get it.

"No, my friend," I explained "I had some deep feelings towards him, that's why I battered him to death. The same happened with the inmates – I held them dear to my heart at that time. That's where you are all wrong! You think I'm a cold and heartless son of a gun. But I am a warm-hearted person and I cherish sincere and truthful feelings to you all!" I smiled.

He was getting it; I could see it in his eyes. He lowered his head in contemplation, and then uttered:

"How can I prove to you that Our Plan is really in service of Mankind? That Satan and all the rest really exist? That we are the good guys?"

"You'd find it extremely hard to convince me of the latter." I hissed. "I'm not sure about the rest. Take me to your people for starters, and then we'll see."

"You are a strange man!" he shook his head "You are practically surrendering. How would you get out?"

"You're so kind," I winked at him, "I like you. You're a caring, giving person. Let me handle this. You just gather them in one place, tell them you won me over and take me to see them."

"What are you going to do? Kill us all?"

I replied honestly, "No. Your games have nothing to do with me. I am not interested. I'll try to convince you to leave me alone."

"You know that's impossible.'"

I sighed, "Then we'll have to think of something on the fly."

We were approaching the city. Now we were driving on the highway. I climbed up a hill and saw the Monster Megapolis city lights. A giant beehive with numerous predators, all stuffed together. Isn't it strange how God acts sometimes and what jokes He considers funny? Yet, who could blame Him for it? He is the World's Creator. He made it, he manages it, and he'll destroy it in his own time. That is his irrefutable right! Honesty and Justice are tools of mass manipulation.

We were driving down the city. Our tail was good – we didn't notice it at all. Maybe they were moving underground?

It didn't matter. I was about to pay a visit to a pack of cannibals. Generally, I don't mind cannibalism – it's just another way to feed. The rest of us eat dead animals, cooked and spiced. Cut and packed against their will, in pain, hurt, cries and agony. From time to time an animal would eat a man, big deal. That's the natural course of life.

But when Cannibals humiliate you, rape, desecrate and torture you for the sheer joy of your pain before they eat you… Then I think they deserve to be treated in the same way. They must be skewered and cooked on a slow fire. They must experience what they do to others. They must learn the lesson, before they 'pass on'. Does that seem cruel to you?

Well, Justice means violent and painful breaking of the will, and punishing the guilty in accordance to the commonly accepted norms. There's justice for you. People remember the pain and suffering the most. Justice is bad and painful.

Do you still want Justice?

Do you wish to be just?

And I?

What about me?

What about me, I ask?

Honestly, I don't give a shit about Justice, it isn't there anyway!

I just wanted to be left alone.

There was only one way to get that.

We were entering the city with all its glory. The sun was rising but the street lamps were still on. Everything around us was going through a transition. The atmosphere was heavy with expectation – the city was about to wake up and fill its streets with noisy people and machines. But there was still a half an hour left before all that. The alarm clocks were still sleeping. The predators were still in their beds, in a lazy semi-hibernated state.

Only the traffic lights were busy on the streets – dedicated workers having no one to regulate yet. That didn't cool their enthusiasm, though.

And the silence… that silence…

It was as if the city was cleaner without the people somehow…

We reached the hotel pretty quickly.

At the very moment we entered the parking lot sidelong the hotel, a vision overpowered me and I almost crashed into a jeep.

All of a sudden I could see everything, without having to turn around or look up. I could see it inside my head. Inside my brain. I could even see through the building walls nearby.

I parked in a hurry and let the vision fill me. Conroy was trying to say something to me. I waved at him to shut up. He wanted to get off. Without looking, I grabbed his left thumb, twisted it and stopped him. I think he moaned.

I focused on my vision one more time.

God, the place was crowded with armed civilians!!! The entire hotel personnel – receptionists, bartenders, bell-boys, and waiters – had guns, hidden in their clothes. There was a room on each floor filled with ten hooded armed men. There were masked shooters in ten of the cars in the parking lot, as well as in the three vans, parked on the other side of the street. Snipers were laying low on three of the roofs of the near buildings. A couple of blocks from here, three helicopters were flying round on silent mode, all full of armed men.

My free favorites were also present – the "Military guy" was in the restaurant, though I didn't quite know where that was; the "Secret Service guy" was in one of the helicopters; and the "Government guy" was hiding in one of the vans across the street.

They day promised to be playful and naughty.

I was focusing on the incredibly real three-dimensional picture in my head for a couple of minutes, just like a Sci-Fi movie.

Then the vision was gone.

They were well-prepared.

A question arose. A whole army just for me? I doubt it! I am a gentle kind of guy, easy to get on with. Meek as a lamb. It takes only one pro with a gun to do me in. Then what?

I turned to Conroy:

"Are you the Head of the Organization?"

"I beg your pardon?" I blinked in surprise.

"Are you?" I let his thumb go.

"Why?" he blinked again.

"It's crowded with armed civilians."

"Well, I told you I had no idea how many will be there." He shrugged and stared at me. "How did you know?"

"I saw it." I waved to cut his questions short – we were losing precious time, "Receptionists, bartenders, waiters, bell-boys… all armed. There is a room on each floor with ten hooded armed men. There are shooters in ten of the cars in the parking lot; in the three vans, parked across the street, too. They have snipers the roofs nearby. A couple of blocks from here they have three helicopters filled with men."

He goggled. He opened his mouth and obviously wanted to ask questions, talk to me… binding more time.

"Don't ask me how I saw it, I just did." I interrupted, "My question is this, is there someone powerful enough who wants you dead? Because, you see, they wouldn't have bothered with that kind of preparation, if it was all for me."

"What are you implying?" he startled "My people are loyal to death!"

"Cut the crap! There is no such loyalty! I'll ask you again, are you the Boss?"

"I take a very important position," he started "and I have a very important role…"

"Why don't you just shut up?" I cut him short "I'm not interested in your Ego. This isn't a board meeting. Are you the boss? You'd better answer me, or I'll let them shoot you!"

He gulped dryly and moved nervously in his seat. Then he answered:

"No, I'm not. I am one of the seniors, but I'm not the Boss of everything."

I shook my head, "Do you want me to tell what's happened?"

"What?" he looked expectantly at me.

"Your people renounced you and sent here a bunch of assassins, because they think you are about to bring a company of soldiers here."

He opened wide his eyes:

"That's impossible!"

"And it is most likely that other killers are dealing with yours subordinates in this very moment. My friend, you're over and done with."

He refused to accept it. His brain couldn't grasp the situation.

I decided to give him a push, "Do you want me to get you out of here alive?"

He looked at me, as if he just fell from the moon. He couldn't utter a sound.

"If you want me to save your ass, I'll need two things from you." I lifted my index and middle fingers in his face.

"What?" he said quietly.

"First, you have to take me to the big boss!"

"OK." He nodded huskily.

"Good." I was about to get off the car. "Stay close and keep quiet!"

"And what is the second thing?" he asked.

"I just told you, stay close and keep quiet."

If you go to a meeting with someone you completely trust and who you thought to be the boss of the people you're heading to see, you are expected to be relaxed and not to suspect ambush and the like. Isn't that right? It is assumed that if there happens to be an ambush, you'll shit in your pants from fear and freeze (hmm, how could one do these in the same time?). The enemy is completely sure about themselves and about you, so they don't expect any other reaction than pants-shitting and freezing, right?

If you take out a gun all of a sudden and shoot the enemy, they wouldn't even have the time to get scared. They could only startle and take the bullet with open arms. There are only two vital conditions, on which your life and your success depend on.

First. You have to be determined to kill your enemy. Each moment of hesitation gives the enemy a golden chance to bend you down, pull down your pants and satisfy their ugly enemy needs on and in you.

Second. There is a big chance your enemy to kill you – if they are larger in number, better prepared and has a longer evil-doing history than you. So they can kill you despite your determination and great shape. So, you have to be decisive and you shouldn't care whether you'll live or die.

Can you do that?

No one can be sure of that. Because, my dear ladies and gentlemen, when push comes to shove, we all usually do one and the same thing – we freeze and shit in our pants. If we still have some time left, we pray to the good Lord (whom we rarely think of in normal circumstances) to spare us, forgive us, help us and save us.

In other words, to have it our way, not the enemy's.

In other words, to screw the enemy.

In other words, everybody else can suffer and die, except us.

Are we just?

So, why does it have to be our way? Why should we win? Why should we survive and beat the enemy? Why should everything happen the way we want it? Why should there be justice, as the books say?

What can I tell you…?

If there's a gun pressed to your asshole, you don't really care about Justice.

I dragged Alistair Conroy, XII straight to the entrance of "The Heart of the City".

Ironic, huh? "The Heart of the City" was full of bad guys.

We entered and nodded to the doorman. There were two women at the reception desk. I stand corrected – there were also some bad girls in "The Heart".

Well…

Too bad for them. For today I'm pretty bad myself.

We headed for the reception desk, where the two very bad girls greeted us with two innocent wide amiable grins. Professionals, I get it.

I also grinned sheepishly:

"Good afternoon, we have a meeting at your lovely hotel."

"If you care to tell us your names and who you are meeting, we'll be glad to be of service." tweeted the blond angle on the left.

I pushed Conroy and he stuttered;

"We have a meeting with Carter Dell."

"Ah, yes," the black-haired fairy on the right jingled. "Mister Carter Dell is expecting you at the restaurant, table nine."

"Thank you." I gave her my "school-boy, just seen his favorite teacher's panties" smile. "That's very kind of you."

"It's a pleasure to be of service." The two gorgeous creatures with perfect smiles recited with one voice.

I grabbed Conroy by the elbow and led him to the restaurant. I moaned in his ear on the way:

"Remind me after we kill everybody, to come back and make them four babies each."

His eyes popped out in disbelief. I patted him on the shoulder and said:

"Just relax and have fun."

Chapter 8

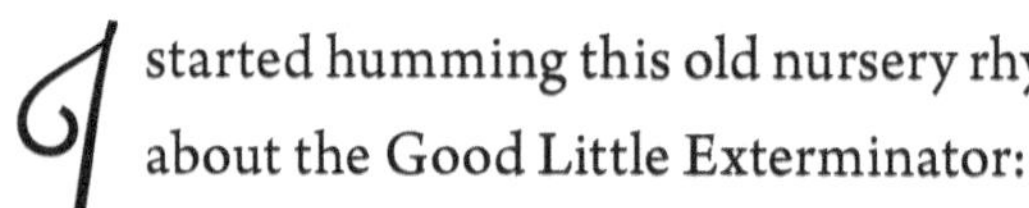 started humming this old nursery rhyme – the one about the Good Little Exterminator:

Oh, my sweet old mamma.
Always sweet and good,
See me in my glamour –
I kill all I could.

Dear bossy father,
See me fight the vermin,
I put all that bother,
To get rid of their burden.

You, my sweet ol' grandma,
Put yourself in my place,

Laugh at all that drama;
I leave no remains.

Hear me, blessed granddad,
Your blood is thicker than water,
Your child is of good stock;
I do enjoy the slaughter.

Alistair Conroy the Twelfth was gaping at me, shocked by my carefree humming. Then he shook his head – he was absolutely convinced I was beyond crazy. I winked at him;

"When we go into the restaurant, you just point this Carter Dell to me. Try not to stand between him and me."

He just nodded.

The restaurant doors were open hospitably. There were heavy drapes with tassels, tightening them in the middle. These people really had style!

The tables and chairs were made of solid wood with exquisite carving and colourful decorations made of whatever the hell it was. The tablecloths were flawlessly snow white with a slight touch of golden threads here and there. I almost wished to forget the whole deal and just sit down and order, order, order...

Hmmm... these places were created with the sole purpose to empty your pockets.

The restaurant was half-empty. The staff was there, though. Heavily armed and cherishing dirty thoughts about me, all right. My vision had already shown that.

It would be interesting to know what the Priest would say about that vision. How could he possibly explain it?

All staff members fixed their gaze at us from the moment we stepped in. I gave them an amicable smile from afar. I haven't brushed my teeth since last night, but I hoped it wouldn't show from that distance.

One of the waiters came to us with a stiff walk (he was trying to hide the gun under his left armpit) and asked us even more stiffly:

"Welcome. What can I do for you?"

I nodded, "Yes, please. We are looking for table nine and Mister Carter Dell."

"Of course. He is expecting you. Follow me, please." He bowed slightly.

Suddenly, the Vision hit me again. It simply overwhelmed me. I saw every single person in the restaurant. Their exact location, clothing, weaponry. All waiters were planted.   They had machine-guns, and on the small wheel-tables and behind the bar I even saw heavy army tommy-guns. I shed a tear and felt the urge to kiss and hug every single one of them! It had been so long, since someone had paid me so much attention! Now

I knew that they were here because of me, not because of Conroy. But why? What was the matter?

There was something fishy about "The Heart of the City".

Meanwhile, the Vision went on uninterrupted. I could see simultaneously both the reality and the vision. They were intertwining in one big picture I was sure would make me mad in the beginning. The events in the Vision were ahead of the real ones with just a second or two. As a result, people's movements started just a second before they actually make them and with a slur merged into their real movements. The waiter, leading us to the table, was literally swimming with a slur before us. The same applied to all sounds. They started just a hint before the real ones and then merged again.

It was slightly irritating and extremely confusing! However...

It was so crystal clear! Someone quickly changed some of my "transistors" up there and in a few seconds I was able to adjust and make the difference between this aura (my Vision) and the real event. It was a fine difference, indeed! Now I could have some fun!

When my Vision started, I lost my balance, pushed a small table, and then leaned on it. Everyone around reached for their guns. I smiled inside.

"Are you all right?" the waiter was "really concerned" about me.

"Yes," I nodded, "I just haven't slept much lately."

We went to table nine, in the most remote section of the restaurant. And there he was – Carter Dell. Sitting all by himself behind this round table, eating something.

The vision went on.

The waiter bowed slightly, with the Vision's slur, and introduced us. I don't recall telling him our names. His voice also slurred with that kind of microphone effect. Then he turned around and retreated.

Carter Dell put down his knife and fork, gently patted his mouth with a napkin, stood up and reached his hand to my direction. The real Carter Dell did the very same things with a second or so delay. I precisely calculated the situation and grabbed his real hand, not the one in the aura.

"Hello," he said with a nice baritone, "nice to meet you."

I waited for the real one to repeat his line and replied:

"It is an honor to meet you in person!" I slightly bowed.

After that exchange of pleasantries, Carter Dell stood from the table and hugged the flustered Conroy:

"I'm so glad you're here, my old friend!" He patted him cordially on the back.

Without my consent or permission, my right hand was in desperate need to throw a few uppercuts in Carter Dell's sleazy hypocritical kidneys; I could barely control it, it kept accumulating so much aggression. Poor Carter Dell! Boy, he had a pretty smart suit! His shoes looked expensive, too... not that I know the first thing about shoes. I only have a problem with his tie, wow, there's something yellowish on it...Gross! And the poor old Alistair Conroy the Twelfth looked as if he had just been hit by a truck. He didn't know who he was or where we were.

When he finished hugging, Carter Dell decided to finish his meal. He returned to his chair and with a wide friendly gesture asked us to join him and sit opposite to him, with our backs to the restaurant. Right! There was a painting on the wall above Dell's head. Some sort of landscape or something. The spot on the wall, though, was bigger than the painting. There used to be a mirror there; a mirror that has just been removed, so that we wouldn't be able to see what's happening behind us.

I smiled inside.

We sat down. A waitress appeared (her gun was in a holster on her inner thigh, under the skirt). I pointed at Dell's plate.

"We'll have the same."

Alistair Conroy XII just nodded in agreement.

"You've got taste." Dell nodded with approval. "You know exactly what to order."

I smiled at him:

"I guess you'd like to ask us a couple of questions, before you start shooting at us?"

He couldn't swallow his bite. He coughed, flustered, then coughed some more. His eyes were red with blood. He couldn't swallow the food and he was about to suffocate. He looked around like a man overboard, who cannot swim. I didn't move. I could see in slow motion how he reaches for the glass of red wine, drinks it and gets better. That's exactly what happened, accompanied by a lot of coughing, wheezing and tears. As someone put it, *"We come in pain into this life; we leave with pain, too."* I would like to add, 'And there's a lot of pain in-between'.

The brutes in the restaurant were making a dash at us. Suddenly, they halted – he stopped with one gesture. That gave them away all right.

He looked me with anxiety and fear – I didn't lift a finger to help him. He could have died there and then, and I did nothing to prevent it. Was I mad? Then he looked inquisitively at Conroy. Despite the tension in his eyes, he remained calm and stone-faced. He would never give up anything. When someone gives you away just like that, patting your back with a smile on their faces, the best thing is to do the same. Despite all master plans he was involved in, Conroy simply wanted to live. That meant, as I have told him, to lay low, keep quiet and trust me. He had just found out that Dell was no friend of his. That immediately made him join my team.

And what about me? What did I want?

I was just having fun with everyone around.

"So, you've discovered the truth?" Attentively and suspiciously Carter Dell asked with great caution.

"Look for the traitor among your people." I predisposed him with a smile.

Dell goggled. Apparently, he was one of those greedy for power people, who like to dictate the rules and behave outrageously; he was playing people like pawns and couldn't bear the thought to be turned into one himself.

"My friend Alistair," Dell started with a rather insecure tone of voice, "who is also a devoted follower, told me you want to join us..." He stared at Conroy to see if the proverbial loyalty was still there.

"Yeah," I interrupted, "he said that, so we could get near you."

He gapped.

"I'd like to ask you one thing," I leaned forward confidentially "can we find a way where I leave this place safe and sound, and you all stay alive? Your fight is not mine. I forget about you, and you forget about me. Well, is that an option or not?"

Anger flickered in his eyes. That was settled, then! No amicable solution to our problem. I thought so! I decided to give it a try, anyway:

"Please, say yes. Or else it gets nasty for all of us. We don't have to force this."

He blushed again. This time it wasn't breathing difficulty, but pure rage. Beams of sweat covered his forehead. Sensitive, aren't we? He clenched his teeth and growled:

"You come here, on my territory, alone with this…" he looked his former "friend" with despise "… and you have the nerve to lay down conditions? Aren't you way overconfident?"

I sighed happily:

"Aren't you way too vulnerable, all alone against me at this table?"

He startled, but quickly pulled himself together and laughed:

"You almost got me there!" he burst into laughter again "You are alone, not I!"

"Am I?" I asked innocently "I see only you. Conroy told me this fantastic story about the devil and the three brothers, but I see you alone. What can you possibly do to me?"

He was furious. That was exactly what I wanted – to push him beside himself and to make him spit it all out.

"Listen, you stupid loser!" he started with a tsunami-like roar, "I have so many people that…"

"I've killed a congressman and a couple of cops." I rudely interrupted him, "and I got away with it. I killed a few inmates in prison, and got away with it again. What could you do to me, really?"

He was heavy as a thunderstorm – pissed, overhanging and dangerous.

"Everything Conroy told you is true!" he started slowly "But you're so dumb (ouch, that hurt), that you just can't see the big picture! And you never will!"

I lifted my eyebrows in silent question.

"We are History!" he went on ominously. "All wars are ours! All discoveries are ours! All politicians, congressmen, ministers, businessmen, judges, police officers, generals are ours! All hookers are ours! We decide who shall rule! We decided who lives and dies! We do!"

"Do you?" I cunningly interspersed with his harangue.

"We do!" he lifted proudly his head 'Our organization is so powerful and strong, that your stupid brain can't process it!'

"So, how many of you are on top!" I asked quickly.

"Twelve…" he said without thinking and then shut up, embarrassed by the easy giveaway.

I nodded. I was already forming a mental picture of that Organization. It was something like an International Mafia, maybe. Why the hell not? We do have international trade companies, so why don't we have an International Mafia? Same difference, any way.

I told Dell, "Let me tell you two things. First, my mother taught me to be a good person and do only good deeds, and help people. Second, my father is a good man, but doesn't have many clients and can barely make ends meet. I have to take care of him, right?"

He blinked rapidly, "What do you mean?"

"You're fighting for a cause all your lives. You don't have the time to enjoy the simple things in life, you know, live a little. Life is a nightmare to you."

He puckered his brows incomprehensively.

"My father's a priest, by the way." I grinned.

He blinked again. Then he suddenly understood and his eyes widened. He opened his mouth and…

We didn't get to eat again, damn it!

I pulled Conroy by the neck and pushed him on the floor. I got up and turned to the hall. I thought, "*If that is your will, oh Lord, take me now.*"

Let's get it over with.

I could see in slow motion how all the bartenders, waiters and waitresses were reaching for their guns.

"Forgive me for what I am." I faltered to myself.

I grinned, shook my head and said loudly:

"Ladies and gentlemen, I came in peace! I must warn you I have no imagination whatsoever and I'm going to kill you all!"

It wasn't that I was faster than them.

I was simply able to see their moves a second before they actually made them. That made me react more quickly. That was my advantage. Was it fair? Definitely not! Would I take it? Absolutely! They wanted to pester me, not the other way round!

The first two attacking …hmm… waiters were planning to neutralize me through violent grips and capture. So dumb! One of them got a kick in the chin, the other a punch in his nose. They flew back and crashed a table each.

I turned to the rest and said, "You should've brought your wives and children! You could have saved me some time, nerves and searching!"

They were slightly taken aback by this statement – exactly what I was hoping for. Fast as a bunny I jumped on one of the tables, then on the next one, and on the next one after that, and so on, and so forth, until I reached the bar, kicking one of the onlookers' face at the same time. Did I mention they were already shooting at me? That's why I was trying to mingle. That wasn't so good – they could shoot one of their own! So, they had to fire at me, and keep each other's backs at the same time. I didn't protect anybody and I could shoot whoever I wanted. Unfair, right? Well, life's a bitch. They didn't welcome me with open arms after all.

I jumped behind the bar, grabbed a machine-gun by the muzzle and pushed it down. The dude was shooting hard, the iron was moving in my hand, burning me. My left hand very impolitely crushed his thyroid gristle. He softened and lay on one side, and I inherited the gun.

The vision was kindly showing me each of the shooters around, no matter if they were standing before or behind me. I didn't know I could see like that!

One of the waiters was about to take the machine-gun behind me. In that precise moment, I was already on my back, aiming. He got three small holes in the chest, before he could act surprised. Meanwhile, another one wanted to shoot me in the face. Again, I was faster with one lousy second and was able to shoot his face. He wasn't a pretty sight, take my word for it!

Strangely enough, the Vision was now showing me only the shooters that presented immediate danger – the ones pointing their guns at me right now. It was making me turn to their direction. The rest were in a blur, probably to protect my brain from burning out. Someone selflessly jumped over the bar. It was a woman. As I was lying down, she landed next to my head. All I had to do is slightly move the guns' muzzle, now pointing at her loins. She looked at me in terror but tried to aim at me anyway. I shook my head:

"Baby, all the world's a porn stage and all the men and women merely porn players!"

I pulled the trigger and looked around for more interesting prey. At least ten muzzles are pointing at me; all of them fired at once. As you can probably guess, my good old Vision projected their actions seconds before they actually happened. I managed to fire three bullets in somebody's chest and to lie down behind the bar. A fast lead river was flowing above me.

In one of the quiet reloading pauses one of waiters cried out like a madman:

"Go to hell, you stupid piece of shit!"

I burst into laughter, "Did I hurt your feelings?"

I rolled over to the left side of the bar, kneeled on one knee and started shooting. I had three down, then I ran out of bullets.

"Give it up, Godrack," Carter Dell shouted, "surrender and we'll kill you quickly and painlessly."

I had almost forgotten about him. I looked at him and he smiled:

"What are you fighting for? Is it money?" he smiled "Is it because of some great love story?" he grinned again "Do you have anything worth living for?"

"You don't need to piss me off to kill you." I replied gloomily and cast a glance at the reloading group, pointing them with my finger, "They were lucky so far! Bullets are more merciful than me!"

I grabbed one of the tables and threw it away towards two of the shooters, standing next to each other. The one managed to jump aside on time; the other was busy reloading and didn't see the flying table before it hit him to the ground.

'The human being is too restrained,' I started loud and clear; the shooters were almost finished reloading, 'in its existence. Think about it – we are merely five – six feet of protein, constrained within itself. We can't fly for instance, we can't jump high, we don't have long limbs and various kinds of natural weapons, like claws, for one,' the shooters were looking at ne in astonishment 'and yet, led by our survival instincts and strive for domination, we all try to use our limited body and mind to a maximum extent.'

I was walking among the tables, accompanying the words with gestures, 'So now I am going to make use of my minimal advantage over you.'

I started throwing the forks and knives I gathered during my speech. I was able to hit a few in the face, no matter it was the blunt ends that hit them. They fired back at me. I kneeled low and started moving between the tables towards Carter Dell in duck's walk. As every other White-Collar worker, he was all panicked. He was standing still next to his table. He couldn't believe I was still standing, and so many of his men were dead. Unlike him, Alistair Conroy was kneeling to the ground and looking round. He didn't think of himself as lord and master anymore; he was starting to consider things and protect himself. Congratulations, Mr. Conroy! Something may become of you one day! That is, if you live to see the day, though.

My vision showed activity outside the restaurant and the hotel. The masked men with bullet-proof vests were heading to us from the floors upstairs. That was the one thing, but there was something else, too. I clearly heard an order, given by the "Secret Service" guy, *'Kill them all! Kill everyone there, if necessary!'*

That order was directed to the "Government" guy in the van, parked across the street. Interesting, I said to myself, I thought he was the leader. I made a mistake. The Government guy on his turn, repeated the order to the "Military" guy, who was somewhere here in the restaurant, but I couldn't see him yet. He replied, "Copy that."

Then he repeated the order to the masked men, running down to us. In that moment, the Vision showed me his location – he was standing in one of the offices behind the bar, next to the kitchen.

That's where you've been hiding, sweetie pie!

I left Dell and Conroy to themselves and went to see the "Military" guy with the same duck's walk among the tables. In the meantime, the waiters were cross-firing everywhere. I quite liked the sound – it added style and thrill to the atmosphere!

A waiter, armed with a machine-gun, popped in front of me, followed by a waitress with a gun.

Why don't they give up already?

I kicked high the machine-gun with my right foot; with my left hand I grabbed the muzzle of the gun and pointed it to the testicles of the soldier with the machine-gun. The waitress dutifully pulled the trigger and castrated her colleague. He fell down with a roar and started bleeding. I drew the waitress closer by the gun and hit her straight in the nose. I took both the gun and the machine-gun. I had to kneel down, because the waiters really wanted to hit this time and did not go easy on their bullets.

I rolled over and fired a few shots below the tables. Five or six waiters fell down – I had hit them in the legs. Okay, they are over and done with. I had only a few left to be taken care of.

Light as a feather and free as a bird, I landed behind the bar with a couple of jumps. I forced open the doors to the kitchen and the offices, then immediately fell on my face. There were black hooded shooters lying down, waiting for me behind the door.

They didn't expect such a quick reaction on my part, so they gave a few shots in the air above me. I used the precious time to count them. There were three men, in the three corners of the room. They had shotguns with clasped butts and were kneeling on one knee.

To hell with all of you! I lifted the machine-gun to the level of my eyes, as I was lying on my stomach. With a single movement from left to right, I shot them in the faces. I waited for a while to see if anybody else from the "Welcoming Committee" would show up. Nobody did.

I knelt and headed for the office where my Vision located the "Military" guy. I grabbed two shotguns on my way. I put one of them on my waist just to be on the safe side.

I was both careful and fast – the hooded men were running down the stairs so fast, I could hear their steps and their breathing!

There was no one in the kitchen. Good. I ran across it with my head low. And there was the office in question! I kicked the door open and curled to the right, away from the door. It turned out to be a great choice – the wall where I was standing a second ago was black from all the lead. Hmm, could I capture the "Military" guy, or should

I kill him right away? No, I want him alive to direct me. Just for now. Tomorrow we'll see.

Meanwhile, my Vision has abandoned me.

I peeped out, took a look at the room and immediately withdrew. The bullets were pouring down the wall again. The three were standing in their corners, and the "Military" one was occupying the opposite right corner. It seemed they were all military, though.

Did I have the time to go back and take a body as a shield? No, I didn't have that time.

The door was in the right corner of the room. So, the most convenient man for me was the guy in the back left corner.

I peered abruptly and presented him a few of my bullets in a very delicate manner. I did the same for the other one in the front left corner. They politely accepted my presents. It was rather risky, because I put myself within the "Military" guy's range. Anyway, I managed to go back into position unharmed. Was that God's will?

"I have an offer for you!" I shouted at the "Military" one.

"Fuck you!" he replied.

Okay, then. I peeped out and he fired right away. He hit the wall again. This time, though, he ran out of bullets in the gun. I could hear him reloading – that was my goal. I jumped from my corner and with a single leap landed straight in front of him. He managed to reload and point the gun at me at the exact moment when I kicked his hand on the side.

Then, he surprised me by crying out, bending forward, grabbing me and throwing me on my back to the floor. He was much heavier and stronger than me. He could batter me to death with just a few punches. He sat on top of me and started hitting me with his fists, screaming and shouting. He was strong, heavy and well-trained, and was not inclined to show me mercy!

For a moment I thought he was going to kill me.

Then I rejected the idea.

I had taken cover with my armpits. He was hitting them with all his strength and shouting something! Honey, you punching my armpits gives me such pleasure and joy!

And the hooded men were coming nearer!

I propped up my back and feet against the floor and lifted my pelvis up with all the strength I could gather. I knocked his balance and he spread his hands for one tiny second. That was the moment I needed to punch a fist in his balls. He cried and squirmed with pain. I gave him a few blows in the face. He softened. I shook him away from me, got up and kicked him in the stomach a couple of times.

After that I quickly removed the belts of the two others. With one of the belts I tightened his hands on the back. With the other I tied down his feet to his knees. He could make only baby steps like a hobbled horse.

He still couldn't recover from the fight and was breathing heavily. However, the hooded ones were at the restaurant, so I commanded:

"Get up!"

Despite the pain and the panting, he obeyed. I helped him. Then I pushed him towards the restaurant. I asked him on the way,

"What's your name?"

"Victor Dalloway" he replied wheezing – he was still panting.

"Now listen! You are my clearance. Before we enter the restaurant, you'll shout to your men not to shoot you. Then we take Carter Dell and Alistair Conroy and get the hell out of here. Is it clear?"

"Yes," he nodded.

He seems to be a steady guy, I like that!

Entering the restaurant, I noticed the hooded men across the hall, taking positions at the exit – half were squatting, half were stooping. They were all ready for action, determined, and slightly nervous.

They spotted us and pointed at us with their shotguns.

"Don't shoot!" Dalloway shouted, "It's me!"

One of them, probably their superior, slightly tilted his head, as if someone was whispering in his left ear.

Then he nodded sharply, replied something and said something to the rest. I already knew what it was. In the moment when they pointed the guns to shoot us, I knocked Victor Dalloway behind the bar. The hoods opened fire.

I laughed loudly, patted Victor on the left cheek and shouted, "Your men just gave you up."

I freed his hands from the belt and shouted again:

"I'm off!" I grinned "If you want, you could show yourself and tell them to stop shooting." I winked at him and dashed back to the office where we came from.

I was sure the kitchen had a backdoor to the street for the garbage, or to the underground parking lot, or the lobby bar of the hotel.

While I was running, I was thinking what to do next. Should I try to run away and hide? No, I can't do that! Now I have them by the throat! Now is the time to break the neck and the backbone of their fucking organization!

Suddenly I had an idea. I was overwhelmed by it, actually. Am I really that smart?

Both the front sliding door and the door to the restaurant were big enough.

Then corridors and more corridors, then you take the staircase down to the underground parking lot, which was pretty large. Maybe four times larger than the open one above. It was quite usual, though – you could park in the open for a couple of hours, wine and dine in the restaurant or visit the lobby bar. The underground parking was used by the actual hotel guests.

I ran quickly along the way, leading from the underground outside. I expected them to reveal my plan any minute now and cut me off. I came out to the right side of the open parking lot. I could see from there the parked van across the street. I saw "my government man" inside.

The Vision, which was lost during the time I was running away from the parking lot, now reappeared. It showed me that the van also contained a driver, and someone on the passenger's seat; there were two more coordinators in the back. They were all armed with guns.

Goody, goody.

It also showed me that three of the hidden men in the parked cars were now out of the cars and just about to notice me. They raised their hands at me as one.

I made a dash to the van. The bullets were friendly patting the sidewalk and the road behind me. I abruptly opened the side sliding door and opened fire with a gun in each hand. I hit the two in the back at the same time. I killed the two in front through the dividing glass. The man from the government goggled his eyes and gaped. I put him to sleep with one blow. I slid the door closed, moved to the front and looked through the back mirror. All parking lot agents were out and running towards me.

I opened fire with my two guns. They took position. I opened the driver's door, threw out the driver and took his place.

I started the engine. Wow, what a loud roar! What a neat piece of machinery!

I grinned and drove off to the hotel, you dig?

I crossed the street at full speed and tires screeching, took the few steps in front of the entrance, and broke the sliding door with a bang. Sorry, it's not my day for gallantry. The hairs on my neck and back were standing on end. I entered the lobby with all my power and glory. I turned right at the restaurant, folding carpets and overturning a few armchairs and tables. I glimpsed at the astonished faces of the receptionists. I grinned and sped up a little more. It's always good to have women watching! I was about to enter the restaurant. There were too many tables and chairs, which could slow me down. I sped up a little more. There were also personnel in bulletproof vests and hoods. They would want me stopped, not slowed down. Probably part of them were searching for me in the kitchen and the offices in the back. But part of them would sure wait for me inside.

I burst into the restaurant all brutal and reckless. I took down four of the hoods immediately. There were four more standing at table nine, where I left Alistair Conroy and Carter Dell. Just perfect!

The hoods aimed at me. I bent down and stepped on the gas. I drove among the tables and chairs. It wasn't my van after all! The hoods opened fire again. The van turned out to be armored. That's it! I'll give them a dose of their own medicine! I took a few more hoods down. Abruptly and with a twist I stopped at table nine. I shot one hood through my open window. Then I reached out and opened the passenger's door. Alistair Conroy and Carter Dell were just staring absently into space.

"Your taxi has arrived, gentlemen." I announced loudly.

Conroy pulled himself together faster, dashed and jumped in the passenger's seat. Carter Dell was still standing venerably and inactively.

"You don't have to tip me!" I shouted playfully.

He closed his mouth and decided it was time to move. He ran and sat next to Conroy. I stepped on it sharply and turned left, heading for the exit. In that moment Dalloway appeared from somewhere and ran over. I stopped. He slid the side door open, jumped inside and closed it behind him. He squatted in the back on my right:

"You have one more passenger," he smiled "but I don't have any money. Can I pay in kind?"

He winked at me.

I really liked this guy! I sped up and we headed for the exit. With a slight twist to the left we took down two hoods, passed through the lobby, tearing down the thick carpet, 'fixed' two more armchairs and a table, and with a mighty roar flew out through the main entrance.

Down on the street, right across the entrance two cars had blocked the road. They were really quick, weren't they? We flew to the stairs (they weren't too many – only ten or so, what's the big deal?), landed on the sidewalk with a crash and with a little jump swept away the two cars. We stepped on the street.

I turned right and decided to check what the van is all about. I said to Conroy:

"See if there are any CDs in the glove compartment, please."

"Do you have anything specific in mind?", he opened the glove compartment.

"Something hard and heavy."

"I knew it." He shook his head.

I didn't just wait for him; I was forcing the engine along the street with a roar. I don't mean I roared, the engine did. I actually think it liked it! I think it liked it a lot! I liked it even better!

I didn't harbor any illusions – with such steady preparation and that many people I hardly stood a chance of getting away – they were going to chase me till the end. On the other hand, they couldn't have blocked the whole city!

Three jeeps were already tailing us in the back, all frightening and dirty-looking. I was thinking about the helicopter and the 'Secret Service" guy in it. Somehow I knew he had an aircraft machine-gun, dying to meet me. I wanted to capture him, if I could.

"There's nothing hard or heavy here." Conroy announced.

"No wonder we beat them so easily." I murmured. "They're all fairies! Turn the radio on."

Meanwhile, I was forcing the car along the street. The city was now waking up and people were leaving their homes to go to work. I was still driving on a back alley, but there were already cars forming traffic. I was waiting with joyful anticipation to finally enter an avenue somewhere here and start the riot!

"Happy times are near." Victor Dalloway mentioned in the back.

The radio caught some station playing Rammstein. I reached and tuned it. The song was called "Fire!" I smiled happily, it was good.

I asked loudly:

"Any suggestions where I should drive to?"

Dead silence.

"Okay, let's drive around downtown, until you figure it out. Victor, could you keep an eye on that guy in the back – he makes too much noise when he rolls on the floor."

He patted me on the shoulder, "Don't worry, I'm sitting on him."

Smart guy! I really like him.

Hold on, there's the avenue, we are about to cut into the traffic! You've probably seen too many movies involving a car chase. The antagonist often honks and switches on and off his headlights to the other drivers. Do you really think that, even if they hear or see him, people would have the time to make him some room, if he's driving like a madman? Do you think there's any place left for them to move at all? I don't think so. The most realistic car chase is presented in the 'Bourne' trilogy. There you could see how everybody is getting in your way and tries to hit you. And they usually hit you! And in the end, you car looks like a smashed can of something, and you look like something the cat dragged in after finding it in a smashed can.

If you want to get involved in a car chase, remember this – Don't do it!

I was considering one more thing, though – our present company would follow us only a little while longer. Because when the shit hit the fan (and you can be sure there will be shit flying around), the police would legally intervene and our tail would have to get out of here. So, we would stand a better chance to get out, too.

I was only hoping I was right.

By the way, the Vision was no more.

Then Rammstein's romantic declarations of love predisposed to some intimate intercourse – with the other cars on the avenue.

I flew out of the back alley, ignoring the red light, and took down two cars in front of us, just for starters. They had bad luck. That happens often in life.

As you probably remember, the van was armored. The "Government" guy was hiding there, remember? That made us almost invincible. Except if the jeeps in the back caught up with us and shot our tires flat. Or, if it turns out they have armor-piercing bullets. Or the guys in the helicopter have some kind of atomic weapon at their disposal.

I turned right at full speed, so that we could cut into the traffic as painlessly for everyone as possible. I was racing slalom among the cars by, truth be told, pushing them out of my way as gently as I could. Every time I touched a car, they stopped immediately and honked at us. I could see in the back mirror the jeeps cutting into the avenue, too. Fortunately, they had to drive round the cars I had hit, which were stopped or parked rather chaotically. That would slow them down, I thought. Oops, I stand corrected. The jeeps drove at full speed and drove directly through the cars.

These guys are not going to give up, even if the police arrived! What the hell was I thinking?

"I'm waiting for your suggestions." I shouted.

The jeeps behind us were hitting, crashing, stepping on and throwing aside cars in a chaotic row. There was the sound of screeching metal, twisting metal, metal impact on another piece of metal, breaking glass, honks and brakes… it all filled the air.

We had to change cars and hide, at least for a while. With this van on our hands we were jutting out in the city as… you know what.

Without slowing down for even a second, I continued my maneuvers ahead. Rammstein were of great help, with their gentle and romantic tales of love and fellowship. I had no other choice but to push and crash the cars ahead of me as gently as I could.

The jeeps behind had no such scruples. They were hungry and ferocious.

Carter Dell and Alistair Conroy were clutching at the seats with their hair on end like cats. Victor Dalloway was grinning like an idiot, squatting in the back, holding fast to the seat backs. Such a freak!

"Go to the supermarket on 36th!" he shouted in my ear, "We can change cars there!"

What a lovely idea! A guiding light! Full speed!

I could hear the police sirens now. We had no time to lose! If they saw us entering the supermarket, they would block it and we would be dead meat. No car would be allowed to exit.

People on the avenue started stopping on their own accord. They had either seen us driving like crazy, or they heard the police sirens. And since it was the morning rush hour and everybody was going to work, the avenue was packed and there was no place to move to. The traffic lights had to turn red sometimes, too.

We had no time! No time at all!

I moved with a mighty engine roar to the middle of the avenue where I could see some free space left. Of course, I took down a couple of more cars. I was gentle, considering how the jeep behind us crashed into them completely. I could see in the mirror people abandoning their cars and running for their lives in all directions.

Did I mention the jeep guys were firing at us? They either wanted to make our tires flat, or they were simply mean. They were hitting the running people.

It was a little bit more spacious in the middle of the road. I could switch to third now.

Always truly committed to the traffic ordinance, I turned right on the crossroad, ignoring the red light, and in the same law-abiding manner headed along the 36th.

The Vision appeared for just a second, showing me the helicopter with the "Secret Service" guy following us from a hundred feet above.

That didn't matter. There it was - the enormous supermarket on 36th Street. A five-story building, with two parking lots – one in the open, the other – underground.

We reached the entrance at full speed. It was on our left, which meant across the street, so I made a sharp turn, hitting the brakes in the same time, and barely found the entrance between two vars. With tires screeching I headed for the lower level of the parking. I slowed down and was just driving about, looking for a prey.

And here it was – a family was putting their groceries into the family Ford. Gas, brakes, and there I was, jumping out of the van, leaving the engine running. I aimed the shotgun to the husband – a man in his forties – and said nervously:

"I'm really sorry, but we have to take your car."

The wife cried indignantly:

"How dare you…"

I looked at the van. Conroy, Dell, and Dalloway with the other guy hanging over his shoulder, were coming. The wife saw them too and poked her husband in the ribs:

"Give the keys to these nice people, won't you?"

I nodded gratefully.

We took the Ford and drove off along the underground exit, all peace and quiet. I climbed slowly and politely (despite the screaming police sirens all over the city) and headed for the main exit. We could hear the sirens at the crossroad, but due to the traffic jam we caused, they couldn't come near us. Did I say traffic jam? Correction. A proverbial chaos of mingled, squashed, and trashed cars. The police would come faster on foot, that's for sure.

The jeeps were probably on the underground level, because they were nowhere to be seen.

We still didn't have time! The family is about to describe the Ford any minute now... if they hadn't fled already.

I politely indicated left, cut into the 36th, carefully avoiding the cars stopped in front of the supermarket, and headed to the direction opposite to the one we came from. We were moving away from the crossroad. I was driving at 25 mph – an exemplary citizen. The shotgun was lying lazily on my thighs.

"We have to change the car one more time. Any suggestions?" I asked.

"The supermarket on 48th is the closest." replied Victor Dalloway from the back. He was holding the "Government" guy in his lap like a baby. I lifted my thumb in approval.

We went undisturbed to the supermarket in question. And again, we drove to the underground level. Now we had more time. Victor opened the door of an old Subaru with his pocket knife. We took it hostage and drove off slowly and humbly about town.

It was time to talk.

Chapter 9

"Why don't you wake up the baby?" I said to Dalloway. "Do you think I did something wrong to him, why is he sleeping so soundly?"

"Nope," he grinned 'He's been awake for quite some time now, but he pretends to be unconscious – he's afraid. I'll give him a little prick.'

I could see in the mirror how my "baby" jumped in Dalloway's feet and hit his head on the ceiling. Dalloway smiled happily,' See?"

"Yeah," I nodded, "what's your name?" I asked our new passenger.

He looked around in silence. I shook my head – every beginning is hard. I wanted to help him:

"Your colleagues have already seen, understood and believed how their own people made them scarce. They gave up all of them. They let them kick the bucket and so on. If we let you go now, the only thing that could happen to you is your former friends kill you. Just like that, as a precaution. So why don't you overcome your shyness and introduce yourself?'

"Daniel Harding," he replied gloomily.

"Okay, thank you." I said.

"So, I have this request to all of you. You know me inside out, and I know only Mister Conroy among you. Please, present yourselves with a few words. As you see, we are united by the common goal not to get killed. So let's sign a treaty, just for a while? For that purpose, it would be best if we get acquainted."

"I am Victor Dalloway. I am in command of the part of the armed forces of the Organization. I have a military rank of Colonel."

"I am Carter Dell – one of the twelve senior members of the High Council of the Organization. I am in charge if its activities in that part of the World."

Daniel Harding was silent. I urged him:

"And what about you, sir?"

He pursed his lips with discontent:

"Daniel Harding. A President's Councilor on National Security."

Wow, that was fantastic!

"Alistair is in charge of subversive activities," Dalloway finished.

"That's not what he was telling me." I showed a carefully measured dose of indignation.

"I have no doubts," Dalloway grinned.

I asked, "What is the purpose of this Organization, anyway?"

Conroy exclaimed, "What do you mean by 'subversive activities'?"

"Well, sedition." answered Daniel Harding.

Oh, he speaks!

"What subversive activities?" Conroy raised his voice, "What sedition? What the hell are you talking about?"

"Alistair, please, it's a subject for a long conversation." Crater Dell chipped in with conciliation.

"You bet it is!" Conroy snarled. "Godrack, stop the car! I demand an explanation!"

I obeyed and stopped by the sidewalk.

"Please, don't stop." Dell turned to me, "I'll explain on the way."

"No!" Conroy almost cried. "I demand an explanation now!"

Dalloway grinned happily in the back.

Carter Dell was begging, "Alistair, please, they'll catch us! Let him drive, I'll explain to you on the way, believe me!"

"No!" the other one shouted "Speak now!"

"Godrack, please drive." Dell urged me.

"Dalloway," I looked in the mirror "have you got any cigarettes?"

"Sure!" he searched his pockets, took out a packet and passed it to me, and then he handed me a lighter.

This Dalloway is a hell of a guy!

I inhaled deeply, let the smoke out and announced:

"Cigarette break! Time for confessions!"

"Dell!" Conroy shouted from the back "I want you to tell me everything! What part of it is true and what – a lie?"

Dell shook his head and sighed.

"C'mon, bro!" I winked "Lies have short legs!"

He shook his head again, "I don't know what part is true and what is not. We were all united around an idea. A Big Bright Idea."

I laughed loudly:

"All dirty stories start with bright ideas. But let's hear it."

"Fifteen years ago the High Council was established. There were Twelve Founders. We all had different backgrounds. I personally, had inherited a chain of hotels all over the World. The other members were industrialists, bankers, landowners… we were all of various nationalities. I am from Texas, by the way."

It was going to be a long story. I drove off slowly. It is always better to be on the move.

"We were all successful men," Carter Dell went on, "we couldn't wish more than we already had. It went about money, prestige, career, everything… we all shared a common feature – we couldn't stand corruption in any of its forms."

I started laughing aloud. Dalloway was roaring in laughter with me from the back.

"It may sound funny to you," Dell said firmly "but that's exactly how it was! It was this idea that united us. We considered the corrupted ones furuncles – a disease that has to be cut out from the healthy tissue! They were hindering the normal way of life everywhere in the World! Think about it and you'll see I'm right! A corrupted cop results in criminals at large. A corrupted politician – money stolen from the ordinary people and used for personal gain. Corrupted ministers – endangering the state in general! We decided to create an Organization which would destroy corruption on a world's scale!"

"You've decided to go against human nature," I shook my head "and to fight against it. Your little enterprise was doomed to failure. It's the same as to forbid people to eat meat or drink alcohol."

"Now I know how deeply misguided I was." he sighed "But back then, 15 years ago, we were all so enthusiastic."

"You mean *you* were enthusiastic." I corrected him.

"No!" he explained fervently "It wasn't just me. I know that for sure! Anyway, with our money and connections, united by the Idea, we created an Orderly Organization. It had branches in every major country.

It seemed so easy…" he looked at me and smiled sadly, "All MPs, ministers, judges, police and army men were just dying to join us; they could hardly wait to be recruited! And the very principle to place a single man to be in charge of many others is extremely conductive to corruption." He shook his head. "Anyway, we created a real military organization, which was supposed not only to eradicate all corrupt officials, but also to extinguish the very concept of 'corruption'."

"Your Organization has one major flaw." I said gloomily. "In order to establish it, you had to buy people. You can't fight corruption by using money!"

"That's true." he nodded, "We were blinded and too enthusiastic. I've always thought that enthusiasm harms any serious enterprise, but… We really were enthusiastic. And you. Alistair, my friend," he turned to look at him, "you are appointed to head the Subversive Activities Department, just like Dalloway said. Your task was the subtle destabilization of the states and the society, so that we could gain advantage and place our people in key positions. And since you were an honest man, we invented your background and made up the legend about the father and his three sons, in order to recruit you. We knew we couldn't buy you, so we came up with a lie. We desperately needed you; we were ready to do anything to get you!"

"I hate you!" Conroy hissed.

"Why did you need him so much?" I asked.

"Alistair is the chairman of the International Association of the Intellectuals." explained Dell.

"I used to be." Conroy hissed "Before you fooled me with me with underhand dealings and entangled me in your vicious Organization! I will never forgive you! You used me all this time! I thought I was doing something significant, something that mattered! In the beginning, every time I heard there were some killings, I had my doubts. But I trusted you and thought you knew what you were doing. I thought there was no other way. Now I understand you have been lying to me all along! And I was lying to my friends and so many other people! Carter Dell," suddenly he said gravely, "From this moment on, I don't know you and I don't want to have anything to do with you! Not even anything remotely connected with you!"

Dell chipped in, "You're absolutely right... I don't blame you for..."

"Blame me?" Conroy shouted "Blame me? You lied to me, you pathetic son of a bitch! You made me leave my family, my home! You made me use and betray my friends all over the World! Blame me? You don't have the right to blame me!"

"We were all deceived, Alistair." Dell turned to him again. "We were all gathered around an idea, and it turned out we were all working for a single man's personal gain."

"And who might that be?" I interrupted tactfully.

"He comes from an old aristocratic background. I should've known from the start that an old aristocrat wouldn't want to fight corruption. Aristocracy hates the common man and stimulates corruption. They go way back together. I should've guessed his objective was to use us to expand and consolidate his Power in the World. I should've guessed he was using us, manipulating us! I should've known we were all instruments in his hands! Pawns! I should have known!"

"Who is he?" I asked again.

"His name is Giuseppe Borgia."

"The Borgias?"

"That's right."

We were silent for a couple of minutes. I was driving around slowly. Just driving along the city streets. People had already started their work day and there was hardly any traffic. So... nothing new under the sun...the same old shit....the same old human desires... power and supremacy...

Could there be any other way, I ask you?

"So, what is Mr. Harding's part?" I renewed the conversation.

"Our link in the local governmental authorities." Dell replied.

"A puppet on a string, huh?" I winked.

"That's outrageous!" the puppet was mad.

"Quit bouncing, you're going to crease my tail-cat." Dell grabbed him tenderly with his claws.

"What about the guy in the helicopter?" I asked.

"What helicopter?" Dell seemed surprised.

"Oh, don't overreact!" I ticked him off. "You know very well what I'm talking about!"

"No, he doesn't," Dalloway interfered "The helicopter and the whole welcoming committee were my idea. The one in the helicopter is Hans Zimmer. He works for... well, for the Secret Services. I thought we were friends and I wanted to secure the premises as best as I could. The truth is, Godrack, there have been a lot of failures in this 'Orderly' Organization lately. More and more distrust settles among its members on various executive levels. I am a soldier. I don't want any failures on my watch! They had been described like some kind of insane killer. When I saw you back then, in the prison, I couldn't form an opinion about you, except that you were a pain in the ass!" he smiled "We thought you manipulated Conroy and won him over. We expected you to show up with an army. We expected you to do all sorts of crazy things, so we wanted to be maximum prepared for anything. What we didn't expect from you was to show up here all alone and beat the shit out of us!" he laughed, "That's what they call irony!"

Then suddenly he became serious and snarled:

"Hans Zimmer, you wicked son of a bitch! I didn't expect you to betray me! You venal motherfucker!"

Daniel Harding moaned. In his anger Dalloway had squeezed him hard in the waist. Now he had to apologize embarrassed.

"And how did you know Zimmer was in the helicopter?" Dalloway was suspicious.

"I saw him," answered.

"How could you see him? He was …"

"I saw him!" I stressed harshly. "Please, I saw him! I'll explain later. Now I have two questions for you. The first one goes like this: don't you want to end this shit and get the hell out of here?"

"I'm up for it!" Dalloway was first "Anything I can do to help! Revolvers, machine-guns, tanks, missiles, or even a cleaver!"

I smiled. I was really starting to fall for this Dalloway!

Alistair Conroy, no longer the Twelfth, announced:

"I am also up for it! I don't want to have anything to with this… hmm… so called Organization! Screw them!"

"I'm also in." said Carter Dell, "I didn't think a good idea like that could degrade that much! I didn't think my friends would betray me! I need some time to think it over. I have to find a new meaning to my life."

Daniel Harding was silent. I didn't trust him a bit. He wasn't that significant or interesting to me, anyway.

"My second question is this: What was the actual assignment you let me out of prison for? Alistair was talking about an army of super warriors, but I just didn't buy it somehow. It's not that it's important, but I'm curious."

"You were supposed to kill the President and the Prime-minister," answered Dalloway, "And we were going to replace them with our people. You were, of course, to be captured, convicted again, and this time really executed, live on air, for everyone to see."

"What," Conroy exclaimed, "You lied about that, too? Carter Dell, you're the ultimate son of a bitch, you vicious prick, a genuine circus freak, you hear me? I know nothing about your bright ideas, but I don't see anything bright in you!"

"I'm starting to think," I hissed "that you're trying to sell me some bullshit." I looked at Dell. "Tell me, what exactly did Borgia promise you, when he gathered you?"

Dell sighed and shook his head. Then babbled:

"A New World Society. And a New World Order. Whatever we think is best."

I grimaced with disapproval and then growled out:

"The Fourth Reich, huh? Good for you! Haven't you read any history books? And you, Dalloway, where are you in this picture?"

"I'm on payroll," he shrugged.

Yeah, simple, straightforward and direct like all soldiers. Also dumb like the rest of them.

"I don't know about you all," I started "especially about you, Harding, because it seems to me you haven't cleared it out for yourself yet, but I want out of this whole story! I can think of only one way to do that. You follow?"

The answer was dead silence. That meant they followed.

Right then I was feeling cattle in a slaughterhouse. My carnivorous masters wanted to have a feast as usual, this time with me on the table, but before that they wanted some entertainment, so they were planning to gang rape me. That's what I call "genuine human entertainment"! Anyway, who am I to judge them? I was only going to kill them all. I mean all of them.

I looked on my right, "Dell, do you really think that the other Council members are enthusiastic, too?"

"They used to be," he replied grimly, "I don't know if they still are…"

"Oh, yeah…Time, money and people don't spare anyone… Okay then, do you think that if this Borgia person ended his days on this earth… the Organization would fall apart and they will let us be?"

"Even if all Council members die," he shook his head, "the Organization already has so many branches that they will continue to exist independently. Once you let the genie out of the bottle, it would never go back in. Never more!"

He thought for a while and then shrugged:

"Actually, only the Council members, Giuseppe Borgia and twenty-thirty people know of our existence. The less important people are just pawns, following orders – they don't know us and they have never seen us. Look, I cannot guarantee you that Borgia hadn't consecrated some of his heirs into it, or that he hadn't hidden documents regarding the Organization somewhere…"

"So…" I summed it up "we have to eliminate … how many in total… fifty people, to get away of this mess, is that right?" I looked at Dell.

He didn't say a word. Then Alistair Conroy exclaimed:

"How can speak with such ease of murdering fifty people?!"

"It's nothing new for all of you!" I cut him off sharply, "Don't act as if butter never melted in your mouth!"

"This is a very serious enterprise!" Dalloway murmured in the back.

"Do you mean you're no good to be a part of it, is that so?" I glanced at him in the mirror.

"Why don't you go fuck yourself!" he snarled out.

"I don't want to be a part in it." Harding said hesitantly, "That's too much for me."

"It's easy for you to sit on your leather chair in your government office and pass sentences, isn't it?" I asked him, "But when you actually have to sweat a little to earn your nice bloody salary, it gets rough, right?"

"And stop fidgeting!" Dalloway ticked him off.

"Why don't you let him sit on the seat?" I asked.

"No, he's okay as it is." He smiled, "Let him be uncomfortable!"

Carter Dell interfered, "I think it's time they started looking for us. Basically, the Organization is not used to having things out of control. And we have been playing on their nerves for quite some time now. They'll contact us, arrange a meeting, and then they'll try to eliminate us…"

"Where could we gather *them* in one place," I interrupted "and eliminate them – first come, first serve, so to say?"

Dead silence again.

"Don't they have regular meetings or something?"

"Only if a serious problem arises."

"Well, don't they have one of those now?" I exclaimed "You are a full member of the High Council! And you want out! Isn't that a problem?"

He nodded vigorously:

"Yes, it is a problem. Maybe the Council will gather to blow me off some time really soon."

"Didn't they blow you off in the restaurant?" I asked.

He shook his head, "No. The blowing off part requires a written notification. If they had killed in the hotel, that would have been a pure accident, not by an order from the Council. A simple mistake."

"Hmmm, how interesting… so where do you usually meet?"

"In an old castle in Germany."

"How far is it from here?"

He looked at me in astonishment.

"What?" I said, '"There are no boundaries now, are there? Nobody is going to check us, especially if we act quickly. I guess, when the Council gathers, they will issue our death sentences and publish our photos in the papers. But the Council hasn't gathered yet, has it?"

"You forgot about my 'old friend' Hans Zimmer." Dalloway added.

"No, I didn't." I stopped the car, pulled the hand brake and got off the car, leaving the engine running.

I went to the back left door, opened it and asked Dalloway:

"Is your friend Hans Zimmer initiated into the Organization?"

"No, I didn't find it necessary."

"So, from the three of you who came to see me in prison, only you and Harding are in the know, right?"

"That's right. Hans just thought he was following an important order – to protect the President from you. He wasn't supposed to know more."

"Good." I hit Harding with my palm on the carotid artery and put him to sleep. "Let's tie him up." I said to Dalloway.

We tied Harding with his own belt and put him in the trunk. I sat on the driver's place again.

"You looked so sophisticated to me," Alistair Conroy murmured from the back, "but you turned out to be such a brute!"

Now, look at that! He's trying to be funny!

"Are you talking to me?" I turned the mirror to catch his reflection, "You stopped referring to me in 2nd person plural? You're hurting my ego!"

Dalloway laughed.

"About Harding," I looked at Conroy again, "He's a government mutt. You have to be brutal to government mutts, because that's all they know! They brutalize the common man in the most disgusting ways! Ah, this reminds, I forgot to kick Harding twice in the head!"

Carter Dell stared at me startled. I got off, went to the back, opened the trunk and searched Harding's pockets.

I took his ID, his cell phone and the wallet. I decided to leave out his lipstick, nail polish and the Vaseline.

Then I got on again.

"Hans won't stop until he finds us or shoots us," Dalloway announced grimly, "I know him too well!"

I frowned and asked:

"What do you think of this: we'll tell him about the Organization, we'll work him up against its members, and he'll leave us be gratefully? How about we just tell him the truth?"

He kept silent for a while, then nodded:

"Yes, this could work. I had told him that we were using you to get to a secret terrorist organization, which was planning to kill the President. And that we let it out of control. Which is true, actually.' He smiled. 'But he'll like the truth even better!"

I nodded, "Okay, here's my plan. First we let Harding go to Zimmer. He'll explain about us and the Organization. Having in mind, that this will be the first time Zimmer hears about it, it will take some time to explain it all. And besides…it sounds rather fantastic – the whole thing about the International Organization for eradicating corruption on a world scale! It sounds like nonsense! So, while they are talking, we go and crush the High Council in that castle. Then we come back and explain the situation to Zimmer."

"Why not explain to him now and let the Council crush him?" Conroy asked.

"Firstly, because we will waste precious time in all that explaining; secondly, he might not believe us, and in all cases he would want to hold us back! I doubt that he'll let us eliminate them! And if we don't do this now, we'll never get another opportunity."

Carter Dell nodded, "Yes, this is true. The other Council meeting may happen in years from now and in a different place. And by then they would have settled our hash."

"Victor?" I looked in the mirror.

"Yes?"

"We need explosives. A lot of explosives! And somebody who knows how to handle them."

"If you're looking for trouble," he smiled ravenously, "you've come to the right place!"

That Dalloway is such a good boy!

And so, we stopped at a gas station and bought some provisions – packed sandwiches, bottles of water, soft drinks and bottled coffee. That would be sufficient to keep us in shape.

Then we headed outside the city and turned down a dirt road. We entered a small forest. Yeah, although people are conquering the whole planet, there are still forests here and there. I don't know if they will last. What a pity! Forests are fresh, nice and full of life; something that can hardly be said about people.

We took Harding from the trunk. He was lying all peaceful and quiet, just like any other government official would do in his shoes. We untied and fed him, gave him some water. We explained that we were going on a meeting with Zimmer in the capital city. And that Harding is our insurance policy, in case something goes wrong. Then we put him on top of a big tree (he climbed himself with just a little help from our side) and tied him to the trunk, riding a bough. We supplied him with all the necessary commodities; even the animals wouldn't bother him.

After that I phoned Zimmer on Harding's cell.

They delayed their answer just enough to trace us. Then a cool, slightly dry male voice answered:

"Hello?"

"Good afternoon," I tweeted, "This is Godrack. I think you remember me?"

"The situation you're in is very grave!" he started heavily.

"Why don't you just shut up for a second and listen?" I cut him off, "I have Dalloway, Harding, Crater Dell, and Conroy! I want to meet you. I'd like to settle this peacefully. Name the place and the time."

"You're in no position to lay down terms!" he snarled out.

"Please, reconsider!" I exclaimed. "I could get the press if you keep being such a prick!"

"And tell them what exactly?"

"That a single person has fooled you all! That you're worth shit!"

He suppressed a growl, took a deep breath, exhaled, pulled himself together and asked:

"What do you want?"

"I want you to listen to me before you shoot me dead."

"Okay," he agreed. "When and where?"

"Tonight at eight, at the pastry shop near Piccadilly, in the central Wal-Mart."

"Okay."

"And keep in mind that I'm holding at gunpoint all my hostages, I have an itchy finger, and I'm quite irritated!"

"So, why wait till tonight?"

"Because I want to know my companions a little better. Bye!"

I hung up and threw Harding's cell near the tree. We waved him goodbye, got in the car and set off. Satellites are great invention, presently working against us. We went to a car dealer's and hired a Peugeot. We bought a couple of cheap cell phones from the shop nearby. I asked my companions to transfer their telephone numbers from the old phones to the new ones. The old ones, though pretty nice, we had to throw into the river.

Then we set off for Germany. No one stopped us – apparently Zimmer was waiting for our meeting tonight and wasn't planning to do anything till then. It was noon. When we didn't show up tonight, he would go to Harding (I was positive he had traced the call) and would have a little chat with him. Maybe he would let our photos on the Internet. Unless we phoned him in that precise moment to say the time and place of the meeting has changed. And this time meet him for real. And this time tell him the truth.

Of course, he could have left to follow the lead from the traced call already. In that case, we were really short of time. Maybe he would rouse all his European colleagues?

Maybe… maybe…

One thought was ringing in my ears, while I was driving. Carter Dell had said that if he had been shot in the restaurant, that would have been by accident. But I 'had heard' Hans Zimmer giving the order to attack me, and this order somehow included Alistair Conroy and Carted Dell. At least that was the impression I had. Was Zimmer really in the dark about the Organization? He must have had extraordinary powers, in order to command a High Council member to be eliminated? Did he fool Dalloway?

I wanted to make it easier, so I shared it with the group.

"I don't think he knows." Dalloway was first to give an opinion. "If he knew, he wouldn't harm Dell! No way! That requires a Council meeting and unanimous decision, doesn't it?" he turned to Dell.

Dell only nodded. He wasn't so sure, it seemed…

"What's bothering you?" I asked.

"I don't know…" he shook his head with uncertainty. "The Organization is not what it used to be… maybe it never was what we wanted it to be? Maybe I already have a substitute? I really don't know…"

"Don't you dare turn sour now!" I scolded him a bit, "There's no other way about it! We go there, blow it all up, and leave! To hell with everything!"

"You should have become a soldier." Dalloway patted me on the shoulder.

I shook my head, "No! I think too much. I'm no good for that job." I smiled to him in the mirror.

Then we stopped thinking and kept on driving in shifts. The car was well-preserved; it could easily keep up with 105-110 mph. Harding's money and our own were enough to fill it up twice more and pay off a dozen road policemen not to give us speeding tickets. And then we were in Germany. We had to a pay a visit there.

As an active officer of the Organization, Victor Dalloway had to be in touch with the major military bases in the world all the time. So we just stopped in one of these emergency bases for weaponry and ammunition. Dalloway made a quick order. The Peugeot could hardly carry all the explosives he took. Are you astonished? It's okay, be astonished. You're wondering how the most powerful people in the world impose their will. With force and violence, of course. That force is human power and weaponry. They have bases and warehouses all over the world. The large bases are clumsy and full of bureaucratic nonsense – everybody knows that. That's why they sustain smaller bases, which are totally the opposite. We paid a visit to one of these smaller bases. Since they didn't kill us on the spot, but served us efficiently and politely, then Zimmer still believed we were going to meet tonight. We had two more hours, by the way. The heat was near.

"Why only explosives?" Carter asked. "Shouldn't we take some weapons as well?"

"They will have enough weapons." I replied coldly, "We'll take theirs."

He goggled. It was his turn to drive and we kept urging him to hurry. It was true he was afraid to drive too fast. But he was the only one who knew where the castle was.

Victor Dalloway said from the back, "If you want a gun, you can take mine."

"No, thanks," he refused, "I don't want any guns."

I shook my head:

"It will be great if you are sure of what you want in the next couple of hours!"

He frowned at me in silence.

We went on driving.

Time was ticking away. The car was trailing along.

I was wondering when Dell or Conroy would start to have doubts and want to run away or just watch the whole thing from aside. I was also wondering if Dalloway would screw me up.

"That's silly!" Conroy announced.

And there were the doubts! It was about time! Better to have them now, instead of when we are already in the castle.

"We are handing them ourselves on a silver platter!" he went on, "I haven't heard of such a silly plan my entire life!"

"Do you have a better plan?" I wanted to know.

"No, I don't, but why should we put our necks into the noose?"

"We won't put our heads; we're going to get them by the balls!" I snapped.

"Who are you going to get?" he exclaimed, "It's only the four of us! They will be more than forty! They will be armed to the teeth! The castle will be secured! There will be cameras and all kinds of traps! I can't believe we are heading there willingly and all alone!"

Chapter 10

"Here's how we are going to proceed," I explained "The three of us will go there openly and will introduce themselves."

"What?" Conroy almost shouted.

Dalloway burst into laughter in the back.

"This is the stupidest thing I've ever heard!" Conroy continued loudly.

"We are going to attend the Council's meeting." I elucidated.

"If they ever let us in." Dell chipped in.

"That's your part of the whole thing," I ticked off "Think about it! In the meantime, Victor will enjoy the pleasant task to surround the castle with explosives. Can you do it?" I turned to Victor.

"I'm not familiar with the castle or with its security system." He murmured thoughtfully, "I'll need some time… You'll drop me off somewhere near the castle with the explosives."

There's a problem for you! I forgot it would be better if Dalloway had a car all for himself. That was a serious lapse. Where could we find a car now? I asked Dell about it, he was supposed to know the area. He reflected on it silently.

"How about a rent-a-car?" I suggested.

"Yes," he nodded, "but we have to turn off a bit."

"Okay, go for it."

Another small but significant detour. This is what happens when you don't fully think things over. Thank God, there were lots of 24/7 car dealers who aren't very picky about who they are renting their cars to. The three of us moved to the new car. Dalloway remained in the Peugeot with the explosives. He would drive behind us and park a few miles away from the castle. Then, while we were sweet talking to our kind hosts, he would place the explosives in the most wicked, mean and unscrupulous way possible. And what would happen later on? Well, just wait and see!

I went to Dalloway's door. I opened it, leaned on my elbow, placing the other on top of the Peugeot, and said:

"Honestly, I don't know if we are going to make it. But I don't care."

He smiled, took out the packet of cigarettes and passed me one. I took it, put it in my mouth and lit it with the matchstick he handed to me. I inhaled, paused for a moment and exhaled. Then I smiled back:

"And truth be told, I'm just happy to be here with you and to work with you, though separately for the time being."

He smiled again.

"Most people would say I'm going mad to trust you with my life, bearing in mind I've only known you for a couple of hours." I went on. "But I like you. I wish we'd met earlier and in a different set of circumstances!"

"Are we going to do something?" He wanted to know, "Or you will continue making a pass at me? 'Cos I really like it!" he grinned happily.

I grinned back and slammed the door in his face.

And so, we allocated the duties and the car placement. I honestly didn't trust Dell and Conroy even a bit. They were the weak link. The one was intellectual, the other – landowner for generations. How did fate bring us together? But there was no other way – I had to stick to them. I wanted to see that High Council in person and I really wanted to see that powerful Giuseppe Borgia. And personally extract all of his teeth… or dentures.

It was almost 8pm. It was time to make a telephone call. I turned to Dalloway, Dell and Conroy:

"Now, here's my plan. So far, you've kept detailed notes with names, dates and time, for all the activities of the Organization. If they refuse to cooperate, you'll give these "bombs" to the press."

"How are we going to do that, if we haven't got them?" Dell asked.

"Try to think progressively," I scolded him nicely "You keep the notes in computers with constant Internet connection, ready to be sent any minute to all the media. You have to cancel the sending every day at some exact time, which changes daily. Only you know the password, you dig?"

Carter Dell smiled:

"It sounds so convincing, I almost believed you!" he smiled again, "They can't call this bluff! I feel well-protected!" he smiled again.

"By the way," I noted, "try to turn this bluff into something real as soon as possible. Because there's a great chance that I would get killed, and you – spared."

"You speak of death with such ease!" exclaimed Conroy.

"Death is just a part of Life." I answered indifferently. "If you think about it, you'll see that there can't be life without death."

"Stop babbling and call little Hans!" Victor ticked me off.

I dialed Zimmer's number. He answered right away and sounded tense, just as I expected.

"What's going on? Where are you?"

"Have you found your friend Harding yet?" I asked.

"I beg your pardon?" he sounded sincere in his surprise "Find him where?"

"You're trying to tell me you haven't taken him down from the tree in the forest yet?" now I sounded sincere in my astonishment; apparently, he really believed we were going to meet him.

"What tree, what forest?" he was slightly irritated, "I am waiting for you in the pastry shop as agreed!"

"We're in Germany." I answered sharply.

There was silence on the other end of the line. It was clear that Zimmer was 'in the know'. I nodded to Victor, indicating that his friend was "dirty". He nodded in response and drove off his car.

"Drive." I ordered Dell.

Hans Zimmer finally spoke on the other end:

"Germany... Don't do anything until I come to you!" and he hung up.

"Call at least three members of the Council and tell them you have enough evidence to disgrace them and hang them in public! Tell them, the only thing you want is a meeting where you will be present as well!"

"If they aren't here already, they won't come at all, if they hear this!" He replied.

"Don't you know your people?" I asked, "I thought you were sure they were already here!"

"I was supposed to report on the successful completion of the operation early this morning. But since Zimmer is 'in' and has ordered my elimination… now I'm starting to think there might be no meeting at all… actually… I don't know what to think…"

"Call the three members now!" I commanded.

All of a sudden I felt as if someone was trying to pull the carpet away from under my feet. I felt weightlessness and despair.

What would you do if you're sure you've deceived someone, and then it turns out he was leading you by the nose all the time?

It was a really nasty feeling!

Carter Dell called everybody on the Council. After he made the last call, he hung up and looked at me with brightened eyes:

"The Council has been summoned. They have just arrived. They are all there. If nothing else happens, at least we'll startle them!"

I started to like Dell, too. It would be such a pity, if he got killed.

"Now they are expecting us!" Conroy announced, "We've lost the element of surprise!"

"Actually, we don't need it." I replied, "We are impudent and cheeky and we don't need the surprise!"

About two miles away from the castle, some armed guards stopped us. They looked professional. Uncompromising. They were informed of our arrival, so they carefully scrutinized us.

"Where's the fourth one?" they asked.

"He was too much of a pain in the butt!" I answered sharply.

He stared at me attentively. The index finger on the trigger trembled for a moment. They let us pass. A mile from the castle the same procedure repeated. We drove for half a mile more and it happened for the third time. Finally we parked the car on a large cobbled parking lot. There were all kinds of expensive vehicles. We continued on foot.

As any other ancient castle, this one had a huge park around it. Enormous trees, gigantic crowns, little meadows here and there, and of course, plenty of lanes for walks, fenced by tall beautifully shaped ornamental bushes. There was also a cobbled lane for vehicles, leading from the parking lot to the castle. VIP only, it seemed.

In the moment we stopped, three soldiers with shotguns appeared from nowhere. They surrounded us politely and escorted us to the castle. That was really sweet of them.

The castle was large and quite real. There was no outer fortified wall or a moat; therefore it must have been a summer residence, a holiday house, so to say, belonging to some high-standing cut-throat. Anyway, it was real and impressive. There was a huge lawn with neat low-cut grass. It was well-lit. There weren't any sentries with dogs doing rounds, but I was pretty sure the basement floor was crowded with them; and there were at least two cameras on each tree around, overlapping their range.

Victor's job wasn't going to be an easy one!

On the entrance of the castle there was a big stone staircase with banisters and lion statues, leading to a large front door. There we were asked to stop and without uttering a single word, they searched us. They took away our cell phones. I was asked about the two rings on my two ring fingers – I replied that one of them was a gift from my ex, and the other – a gift from my present mistress. They bought it, slightly jealous.

Our three present companions gave us away to a couple of new ones and withdrew. The two new ones, again armed with shotguns, poked us through the castle.

I noticed it was full of people – masked people. Was that a fancy-dree ball? Bah, aristocracy!

I asked Dell about it. He just shrugged. That man was good at nothing, really!

Let me describe the castle a little bit. You'll see it was worth it. We crossed the large main high-vaulted entrance of big hewn stones and entered something like an entrance-hall ten by ten with two winding stone staircases, leading to the second floor, on the tow side walls. There was a door in each of the walls next to the staircases. There were a few stone steps right ahead of us, leading to a second front entrance, smaller than the other. The first entrance had iron doors, and this one had wooden doors with iron plates.

We crossed the second main entrance and entered a huge ballroom. It was the size of a football field. There were ten heavy columns from left and light, which supported the whole construction. There were these long, heavy, red …hmmm…curtain-like things, hanging from the columns. Five gigantic chandeliers were hanging from the ceiling. They had lamps instead of candles. The floor, the walls, and the columns were faced with brocatelle. I don't think there was any white in it. They had to live up to their reputation and couldn't use such a simple and common thing! There were antique wooden tables, chairs and sofas along the walls. And they were covered with heavy thick colorful fabrics. They were all occupied by masked people.

The entire second floor was jutting out above the ballroom, terrace-shaped, surrounding the whole place. I wasn't able to see anybody there, but obviously that was the VIP lounge. If I had a rapid-fire weapon, that's where I would start.

Slow and soft music was playing. A dozen couples were swirling delicately around the room. Indefatigable waiters were buzzing around like bees.

We passed by two boys, fighting over a cookie or something on the floor near a table. I was surprised by the violence in their expressions. They weren't playing around. The one managed to punch the other in the face a couple of times and take the cookie. He sat on the floor with his back to the other boy, and started eating his trophy. His rival flew into a rage. He reached and grabbed a fork from the table. He growled out and aimed at the winner's neck. I reached out and stopped his hand. He was twisting like a warm on a hook, fulminating like an adult. I took away his fork. He sat on the floor crying in his rage. He tried to bite me on the leg; I shook him off. He wasn't even five.

I grabbed a hand, heading straight to my face. An angry lady wanted to slap me with her claw. She was dressed in a scarlet outfit, resembling a butterfly, with wings on the back. It was to cry for! Probably that was his absentminded mother. I smiled at her. She swore at me. In the next moment, my hand was squashed in the vise paw of her pedigree husband. He was too big for the expensive suit he was wearing. He was bulky, fat and was panting with fury. He smelled of liquor, sweat and perfume. A bouquet for connoisseurs!

It was not until then that he looked at us and saw the rest of our merry group. His anger turned to astonishment. Then he noticed the weapons of the guards. His astonishment now turned to fear. He let go of my hand and stepped back. The mother swore at me once more. I looked down at the children. One of the boys, with half a cookie in his hand and a full mouth, was pointing complacently and mockingly at the other. Contrary to what I had expected, the other boy didn't cry. He was looking at me in silence with an adult-like viciousness. You, little snake!

Yeah… that's the Society of the powerful and successful for you… 'The High Society'! The young generations there are taught from a very young age to oppress the weaker and to take anything they can from others. That's the rule. That's their way of life. That's their philosophy. That's their religion. That's how it has always been and that's how it will always be!

We passed them by.

We went across the large ballroom. On the other end we were transferred to another pair of guards. We went through a door and passed along a few corridors. We didn't go upstairs, which was too bad, 'cos I like to see the world from above.

Finally we reached the sacred place – the conference room. The hall of the High Council!

There they searched us thoroughly again. I had to explain about the rings all over again. And again, they were jealous of me. Human nature, that's all!

A heavy two-folding wooden door opened for us. I looked behind my back – there were ten armed guards. Good! I let Carter Dell and Alistair Conroy pass before me. We entered the hall.

There was a big round wooden table in the middle. How romantic! Eleven men were sitting around it and turned to look at us as one. The twelfth chair was empty. Slowly Carter

Dell headed frivolously to his chair. He stood by it without sitting on it. The two wings of the door closed behind me with a bang.

A hush fell over the room. I took advantage of that and looked around the room. It was about ten by ten ft. there was a smaller door on the other end. The round table was placed in the exact centre of the room and was about three ft. in diameter. The hall had no windows, which meant no outer walls. Some big antique paintings were hanging on the walls. There were four sofas along the walls too. A reproduction of the famous Sketch of the World was painted on the ceiling – the one in which the Holy Inquisition was pulling the strings from high above. Churches, emperors, societies and peoples. God was shoved somewhere in the corner and tried not to hide from Loyola's harsh eyes.

I smiled unintentionally and shook my head. Then I gazed at the High Council members. They all looked like ordinary men. Between forty and sixty. All dressed in simple dark-grey suits with bowties. Most of them had the same formal haircut and musketeer goatees. I wondered whether I should crash their heads open or to sit with them, have a glass of wine and share some dirty jokes about the queen.

It was hard to believe that these normal, even meek-looking men are buying and selling politicians, ministers, judges, district attorneys, MPs, police officers, army men, assassins, and hookers... And all because of some twisted "Bright Idea"? The painting on the ceiling was very suggestive of the "Bright Idea". Let's play God... No, no, let's get rid of God, let's shove him in the corner, because we are smarter and more capable than him, and we can fix his mistakes. We'll repair his imperfect World. We are something more than God himself!

Fie!

Carter Dell announced solemnly in a loud voice:

"You all know why we are here..."

"You're not welcome here!" a bold man in the far end of the table ticked him off harshly. "The way you invited yourself here, speaks for itself! You are a traitor and blackmailer, Carter Dell! We let you here only to vote by a show of hands your exclusion and then to execute your death sentence! Now, shut up and step away!"

Dell turned pale swayed a little. He was finished. All my talk about discrediting insurance policies was pouring down the drain. All it took for him to forget all about it was to hear the words of the spokesperson. He turned round and looked for me like a drowning man clutching at a straw. I nodded to one of the sofas – I wanted him to go there and sit down. Staggering, he collapsed at the nearest one.

Conroy whispered:

"Those nasty sons of bitches!"

The spokesperson's eyes fell on me. He was used to giving orders and usually people obeyed. His kind was the easiest to stamp down.

"Come here!" he barked.

I smiled inside and stepped slowly forward. The people around the table were following closely my every move. Wow, I had no idea people admired me that much! I feel such joy!

I stood by the empty chair.

"That's enough!" the man said harshly.

I stopped and casually put my hand in my pocket. The man bit his lips in hidden anger. He pulled himself together and decided to show me in a polite way that I was nothing compared to him. Looking disparagingly in the blank space next to me, he spoke as if I wasn't standing right there:

"We've read your file. It's surprising how a freak of nature can live that long and get that far."

I was rocking slightly: heels – toes – heels – toes… I fixed my hair.

"You belong to some sheep pen – to herd on the sheep!" he went on, "You're living proof how people get negligent of their work and let someone like you wandering aimlessly and uselessly among normal people!"

I was looking at my nails; they needed to be trimmed. I had to do that after we left this place.

"You're proof of how sometimes, due to the unfortunate concurrence of circumstances a low-intelligence primate can sneak into a rational society."

My right ear was kind of itchy. I scratched it. Could I have some form of fungi? I really needed to see an ear doctor.

"Do you have anything to say before we execute you?" the guy asked me sarcastically.

My neck was stiff. I cracked it a little bit.

A looked the self-centered prick in the eyes for the first time. Calmly, ruthlessly and coldly. In a couple of seconds he gulped nervously.

"Your health problems," I pointed at him with my right index finger, "will allow you to play God for a really short period of time. After that your existence will turn into torture, pain, fear and devouring handfuls of pills every day. And since you're a coward by birth, you'll day a thousand times every day."

I smiled. He was shaking.

I went on with marked indifference, "And then your friends and associates will kick you out of this hall in a hurry and without honors. When this moment comes, think of this evening." I smiled again.

He reached for the glass before him and quickly gulped. Then he reached to a hidden place under the right arm of the antique richly-carved gilt chair. I see the alarm button. I was wondering where it might be.

In that moment ten guards with nervous index fingers, evil looks and butcher's habits burst in from the two opposing doors.

My sweet friends! I was surrounded by TLC. That's what I call taking care of the fellow man!

I was prepared to be overwhelmed by the Vision any minute. No signs of it so far. That meant the situation wasn't critical yet.

"This guy is bothering us," the spokesman nodded to me, speaking to the head of security, "you will remain here during the meeting. Then you will forget everything you've seen and heard."

The other nodded sharply in a military manner. He glanced at me with hostility and came to me. He stood right in front of me. His nose was just a few inches away from mine. He stared at my eyes, then slowly moved his lips and clicked his tongue. His gaze was steel-grey. He looked absolutely uncompromising, unscrupulous, and capable of no remorse. He smiled faintly. His smile could cut though glass.

"You can forget about it," I said, "I don't kiss on the first date."

His smiled slowly turned into a frown, suggesting all kinds of sadistic forms of entertainment.

"Patton," the spokesperson said, "step back! Your order is to neutralize him only if necessary!"

The army man before me followed the order with distinct dissatisfaction. I blew him a little kiss in the air. By doing that, I surely grabbed his full attention.

The Council spokesman took another big gulp. I looked around to check where he got his drink from. Aha, on the right of the sofa, where Crater Dell was sitting stiffly, I saw a portable bar with great variety of choice. Shall I pour myself a little something? No, I'll wait for Dalloway and then we'll have a drink together. Oh, yeah.

"We'll have a good talk later, you and I," Patton snarled behind my right shoulder, "you're going to sing for me!"

Obviously, he was planning to torture me. I hate these guys! I replied wickedly:

"I'll sing for you, if you 'blow my whistle', darling." I gave him another kiss in the air.

"Patton!" the spokesman shouted gravely. "Cut it out!"

"Yes, sir!" replied my new friend – now he was planning to slowly eat me alive for sure.

I turned my attention to the High Council. When would Hans Zimmer drag along? Would Giuseppe Borgia grant us with his presence? If they both came, they would solve all my problems in one go. I would be so happy; I could kiss them… before I kill them both.

"As you know," with a more or less balanced voice, the spokesperson started solemnly, "we had to call an emergency Council meeting. We have a couple of points in the agenda. The first one is Crater Dell's treason. By coming here, he made the matter easier for us. Otherwise, we would have given him a judgment by default. Now, he would be able to hear his death sentence in person." He looked at Dell, "Stand up and approach us!"

Without me seeing, Dell had grabbed a glass, poured some liquor in it, and gulped it down. Way to go, man! Now he poured himself another one and took a sip. He neither stood up, nor approached them. He simply said, still sitting on the sofa:

"I haven't betrayed you! You blew me off in the hotels' restaurant! You've issued my death sentence even then!

Cut the crap, won't you?" he coughed and fixed his tie casually. "I'd like to say to all of you, members of this … hmm…Council, that as of now, you mean nothing to me!"

I could hear some astonished exclamations. Dell ignored them and went on:

"The way you gave me away, speaks enough for the nature of this… organization! I could see I've been used and lied to for years!"

"Silence!" the spokesman almost shouted, "You are in no position to speak about the High Council or the Organization! You are a trait…"

"Stop babbling about!" Dell was getting really angry, "High Council, Organization… It's all bullshit and nonsense!"

I could hardly stop myself from laughing. I wished Dalloway had been here; he would've enjoyed this very much. Conroy was smiling faintly. Patten was clenching his teeth so hard, I was worried he couldn't be able to open his mouth after that.

"Dear former associates," said Dell looking at straight in the eyes of each member, "Do not harbor any illusions. The purpose of this … organization is to serve for the personal gain of our dear 'benefactor' Giuseppe-fucking-Borgia, as well as a few of his close bootlickers. I was sacrificed today. Tomorrow it's your turn!" He sipped from his drink; I wondered what he was having.

He was brilliant anyway. He said it right in their faces. I really started to like Carter Dell a lot.

"If you don't believe me today," he hiccupped and pointed at them, "tomorrow, when they pull down your pants and bend you, you will!"

Oops, he was getting really drunk. I was afraid he was going to make a fool of himself and me, too.

"And beside, FYI," Dell announced with an air of importance, "I'd like to inform you that I've been keeping notes with names, dates, times and places for years. These notes are kept in a computer with constant Internet connection, ready to be sent to all major media and the police. I have to cancel the sending every day at a different time. I am the only one who can cancel the command. So, if you harm me today, your sorry asses will show up on television tomorrow!"

Well, he went too far, I was cutting him off!

Before anybody could say anything, the door behind me opened with a bang. We all looked at it, quite unwillingly. Hans Zimmer was standing on the threshold. He was panting and full of evil intentions. With a stare like this, who needs a machine-gun! A couple of sweaty streaks had dried on his face, resembling glazing on a pastry. Lovely! You almost wished you could take a bite! Even more, he looked extremely sexy in that uniform!

Some more brutes were eager to come in, running about in creative chaos. I could see in their eyes this firm determination to re-paint the walls with the color of my intestines. The feeling was mutual.

The other door burst open too. Some guy was pushing an old man in a wheelchair. Behind them, another guy was pushing a mobile cabinet on wheels. There were all kinds of hoses, cables and medical equipment in it, leading to the old guy in the chair. One of the hoses was stuck in his nose. Two others went in his pants. A couple of cables were prodding the right side of his collar. An oxygen set was covering his face. Apparently the cabinet was in fact life-saving equipment.

I shook my head – that was the embodiment of all deviations of Power. They pushed him near me. He was breathing with difficulty, holding the oxygen set on his mouth. Each day of his life was a gift! No… Each day of torture was imposed on him!

A handsome young man in a suit knelt on his left as a trained puppy. The old man kept staring at me. His gaze was like…Let me describe it in details, it's worth it. There was no weakness. No pain. No anguish. No fear. No doubt. These eyes wouldn't blink if they saw a machine-gun at point-blank, or the stare of a ferocious lion. These eyes wouldn't blink, even if someone started cutting him piece by piece. This man wouldn't bow to no one! He had a Warrior spirit I've never seen before in my life! His eyes were staring as if he had already seen everything in this world. Many births and many deaths. A lot of good and a lot of evil. He looked as if he was present at the Creation and would live to witness the Judgment Day. This stare was radiating such superiority and such frightful power; you couldn't help but hope this man would never rise from his wheelchair!

I wondered what he was like when he was still able to walk!

The old man removed his oxygen set. He spoke surprisingly loud and smooth in Italian. The kneeling man was interpreting for him. I see, that was his job. He was translating with a sentence or two behind. His voice was a bit shaky, in total contrast with the mighty voice of the old man.

I felt that if Giuseppe Borgia looked at me and pronounce the words loudly, he could knock me down as if he punched me in the chest!

What did Giuseppe Borgia have to say to me? What were the words of the Father and Creator of the Organization, entangling the whole World in its web?

"Your actions are impressive." He started. "I have to admit you caught me by surprise! I didn't expect you to come this far. I didn't expect to survive in the hotel, even! You're very skillful!" he paused for a moment and wheezed. "I don't like it, but I have to admit I like you!"

He tried to smile. It seemed he hadn't done for a long time – he had forgotten how.

I smiled politely back.

"Just out of curiosity..." he started coughing and put his mask for ten seconds; each moment was a real torture for this man, "just out of curiosity, how did you manage to beat my men at the restaurant? We've seen the tapes of the security cameras. You are unique and very quick! But the more impressive thing is that you've always acted with great precision without a single unnecessary move; always slightly ahead of the others. It was as if you could foresee each move they made. It was as if you could see all around you!"

I smiled modestly and looked down:

"My Lord was guiding me." I answered bashfully.

He smiled, this time successfully, but when he tried to laugh aloud, coughed again and had to use the oxygen set again.

For a moment I almost felt sorry for him. But only for a moment. I rejected the idea. He didn't feel sorry for anybody or anything. So what if he had to live his life in this wheel chair and be kept alive thanks to this equipment? He was in pain, it was true. Each breath was a torture. And he would never get better. Never! And he was most likely doomed to die in incredible pain, because his spirit was so high. But did he devote his life to charity work? No! He had a heart of stone. Make that last one "marble"!

He restored his breathing more or less.

"You're just like me." He looked at me. "People and life mean nothing to you. You also kill without giving it a second thought!" he smiled quite successfully, "I like you. Why don't you join me?"

Those last sentences caught the interpreter by surprise and he startled. He looked at his Master with pure astonishment. He slowed down the translation. The old man reached with his left hand, grabbed him by the right wrist and squeezed it hard, it cracked! Tears appeared in the young man's eyes. He couldn't suppress a moan. What a nasty son of a bitch! He was still an active killer! I couldn't squeeze anybody's hand like that! What other surprises was this old lame beast holding up his sleeve?

The youth swallowed his tears and finally translated Borgia's last words.

I smiled:

"And you'll appoint me as what?"

"Just join me." The old man smiled, "You'll do whatever you like."

I smiled again. If I keep smiling that much, there's a real danger I could turn into a good man. I shook my head, and then asked:

"May I have a drink?"

Borgia generously allowed it with a gesture. I went to Carter Dell. The members of the High Council whispered quietly, trying not to annoy their Master. They were obviously redistributing positions, posts, privileges, and territories. Those assholes!

Dell was helping himself with yet another glass:

"Stop drinking!" I scolded him. "Quit now! What am I going to do with you later?"

"You leave me alone and that's that!" he replied boldly.

I shook my head and went through the bottles. They were all of good quality. I spotted a bottle of 'Bombay Sapphire' and grabbed it. I poured some in a square glass – it was the only one left. I poured quite a lot – about 200ml or even more. I was about to talk a lot. Moreover, that gin could serve me well in some other circumstances.

"Tell me a little bit more about your Organization." I asked Borgia.

"All right," he agreed, "I'll tell you some of the well-known facts, just to convince you. Sit down." I went and sat next to Carter Dell. Conroy joined me.

Chapter 11

"The moon peers down on a diseased world...
There is no cure for the disease, an entire race
walks mindlessly into destruction. Not even a
man of colossal power, would be able to prevent
the inevitable."

Seijuro Hiko

Borgia lowered his head, as if to gather his thoughts. Then he looked at me and spoke with his deep mighty voice, while the interpreter was translating shakily:

"The High Council was established fifteen years ago. But actually, the Organization existed a long time before that." He smiled, knowing he had already caught my attention. "In the story that Alistair told you there is some truth, though not exactly as he knew it. I'll give you some information about the Organization's activities which even the Council members do not know."

The members of the Council gasped as one and started whispering. Borgia smiled – he seemed to get the hang of it.

"What I'm going to tell you won't leave this room, don't worry," he turned to the council, "because he will either join us or die here." He turned to me and smiled; he couldn't fool anybody with that smile. "The Organization used many names through the centuries. Here are some of its most significant acts. Let me start with the Three Crusades. The Organization was their heart and soul, as well as financial supporter. You may not believe me, but I have diaries to prove it. If you join us, I will let you read them."

The Council members whispered again, apparently none of them had read these.

"Then I'll mention the defeat of the Turkish Armada at Lepanto. All captains were appointed by us. The action plan was ours. The financing was ours, as well. Of course, the profit was exclusively for us; it was we who secured the victory, wasn't it?" He winked at me. "Establishing an Israeli state was also our idea, although things got slightly out of control." He clicked his tongue with discontent, 'Soon we will restore the order.'

He smiled; I wished he would stop smiling I had chills on my back, 'Shall I mention the two World Wars?'

"Master," the Council spokesman said timidly, "is it wise to disclose so much information about our Organization? What if…?"

"I'd say your position is very convenient," Borgia slightly turned to his direction and cast a sharp glance on him, "it doesn't require any extraordinary abilities or skills, it doesn't bear any important responsibilities, either. But if you still want it, stay down and keep quiet!"

The spokesman hushed up, lowered his head and gulped dryly a few times. Borgia turned to me again:

"I apologize. So, about the two World Wars. They were necessary. People had to be cleansed from all the filth among them. The weak futureless sprouts of poor quality had to be removed. The Societies had to be purged! People's view of life had to be cleaned. I think we managed well.' He smiled again. 'Do you need any more details?"

I was standing with my head down; Bombay Sapphire in one hand, searching in my pocket with the other.

"You'll probably ask why the Organization never surfaced, despite its active role and world significance, and why nobody knows about it, except the results of its acts?"

"Maybe I was planning to ask about it." I answered vaguely.

"I will answer that." He smiled one more time, I stopped counting. "People are easier to manage, when they don't know they are being managed. Think about it. What do you know about the CIA, for instance? Nothing much."

"Their headquarters is at Langley." I replied.

"Who says so?" he exclaimed happily. "Never mind. I meant that the CIA decided the destiny of millions of people, and the only thing you know is their name. You didn't know that much of our Organization till recently. Do you understand?"

"Yes." I nodded. I didn't feel like drinking anymore. I shook my head.

"So, what is the purpose of this Organization?"

"There has to be some Order in the World.' He replied, 'Otherwise, people are prone to anarchy. I'm talking about World Order, not order in the individual states. The countries behave as classmates from the same school, but from different grades. You know, some are first graders, others are in second grade, some are third graders, and some are seniors. You can guess how their characters, abilities and desires are quite different. There's no need to explain any further – just watch the news. Do you understand the purpose of the organization now? We keep the balance of world level."

I was silent. True, he spoke of real things. But… something inside me didn't let me believe him. During my years of experience I had learned that my inner voice was rarely wrong.

"I'll tell you when and where the archetype of the Organization was created." Borgia announced gravely and looked me inquisitively.

"Tell me." I shrugged.

"It was created by the emperor Vespasian, shortly after he was proclaimed to the throne in the year 69," he took a deep breath from the oxygen set, "to restore the order in the Roman Empire, which wasn't in its greatest shape. That was the 'Year of Four Emperors'. A brilliant military commander, Vespasian understood the necessity to rule with 'with and strong hand'. Because of him, the Empire was financially and military stabilized. Due to the Secret Organization he established. Of course, it went by a different name at the time. Do you know that Vespasian was one of the very few Roman emperors who died of natural causes, although he participated in many battles and created a lot of enemies? Think about it for a while!"

I was thinking. I looked at the gin in my glass. I didn't feel like drinking anymore. Why did I keep holding it in my hand then?

"Vespasian knew the human nature extremely well." Borgia went on "He started building the Coliseum – one of the greatest human achievements of all times. He knew that human aggression and blood-thirst should be channeled through war or at the Arena, or else we'll simply annihilate one another."

I shook my head.

"Look upon the Organization as a Coliseum on world level and you'll understand its essence and why it is necessary!" Borgia finished with a serious tone.

"Maybe you're right." I answered vaguely; I was suddenly void of any desires, nothing interested me anymore; I didn't even care what would happen to me from now on.

I left my unfinished glass of gin on the portable bar by the sofa, where Dell and Conroy were sitting. I looked at both them without actually seeing them.

I didn't like what I had just heard. I didn't like it mainly because I sensed it was all true. There are many facts about human nature that I don't like mainly because they are true! What did the Romans say? "Bread and entertainment"? Who am I to go against nature? Fuck it!

"You invite me in." Again, I put my left hand in my jeans pocket; I shook my head indecisively and started slowly walking around:

"Truth be told, it sounds tempting. There is a lot of truth in your words about the World and the people, I admit that." I continued walking around. "I can't deny that. To be a part of such significant enterprise and to participate in making the world's history… I've never thought I could be offered such an opportunity! I've never thought my life and work could be of such significance! I never thought I could be that important! It makes me dizzy…"

"Why don't you rest for a few days and think about it." Borgia advised me kindly. "I give you all the time you need to make up your mind and prepare. Till then, be my guest here, no matter what your decision will be. My house is your house!" he declared solemnly.

"I am a simple guy." I looked at him "I see things in a simple way. Alistair's late brother," I nodded to Conroy, "promised me a sweet job, an office job. I didn't have to do anything all day, just drive Mercedes cars, receive solid governmental salary, and fuck innocent school-girls if I want to. Honestly, I barely had the strength to refuse him."

Conroy frowned nervously. Borgia smiled faintly. My right hand had the incontrollable desire to level him with the floor. The Council members looked at Conroy. He nervously crossed his legs.

"After that," I went on, "I had some tempting offers in prison, too! Every other inmate wanted to fuck me. I've never enjoyed that much attention before! I felt loved and acknowledged. I could hardly refuse them, either. Really! It's as they say, *'Once tried a man's touch, one would never look at woman again.'* Right?"

I could see smiles on some of the faces here and there. Making progress, huh?

"Then three guys came in prison," I went on, turning to see Hans Zimmer's face, standing grave and harsh by the door behind me, "and offered to get me out of there, if I bend a little, of course. Well, I couldn't refuse them! Moreover, there was this pretty lady who promised me the world in her eyes!"

Borgia smiled (I think he had made some improvement in that) and nodded to one of his people. The guy left the room. Where was he going? Was he going to fetch Elizabeth for me?

"Later, Alistair Conroy wined and dined me, offering to recruit me. I had to refuse him flatly and even harshly."

I looked at him. He smiled faintly for the first time since we got here. And it was all because of me! I greeted him with thumbs up and continued walking around.

"Then, in 'The Heart of the city' I was welcomed with open arms, which almost brought tears in my eyes!" I looked at Borgia – he looked serious and kept a straight face; he had his oxygen mask on.

"And all this time," I kept walking "they kept telling me these great tales, all different from one another…" I stopped at stared at Borgia, "I'm inclined to think that you are the one, telling the Truth here!" I went and took my glass of gin, and then sipped a little. "This gin is superb!" I raised my glass and greeted Borgia.

He nodded behind his mask.

"There's only one little problem." I lifted the glass to my eye level and examined it thoroughly.

"What's that?" Borgia rumbled and the interpreter translated his words with trembling voice, still holding his hand.

"This is not a gin glass!" sharply, rudely and gravely I answered; staring in his black eyes with fixed determination.

A shadow of anger darkened his face. He knew I was playing with him. He opened his mouth to speak, but I was faster:

"I'll tell you what the problem is. The problem is that all of you are sick bastards! You suffer from an inferiority complex and you try to deal with it by an indescribable thirst for power! You feel complete only when you dominate other people, as rough as possible! When you are in a position to decide their fate! When you order this and that one to die, only because you felt like it! When you get this and that one out of prison to do a job for you and then to throw them away! When you give a percentage to drug dealers, because you're planning to make them pull your chestnuts out of the fire! When you put a hooker in some state official's bed, so that later you could bend him and ride him as long as you like, and then replace him with somebody else! When you eliminate or buy congressmen, ministers, the military, and judges and so on…"

"But that's just Life!" Borgia smiled at me. "That's Life, my dear! Haven't you grasped that already? This is

Life, there's nothing more to it! This is Life and these are the People living it! Or maybe you prefer to live in a lie?"

I looked at him gloomily:

"I think otherwise." I said indifferently, "I think life can be pleasant enough without you, sick brats, in it! Because there's no cure for your sickness!"

I could see in his eyes the firm determination to kill me. If I were within his reach, he would probably have grabbed me by now.

"I offered you the World," he screeched like metal on metal, "and you spit in my face! No one has ever tried that before! You have no idea what's ahead of you!" His eyes resembled the mouth of a heavy machine-gun.

"And you expect me to join this madness?" I looked at him coldly, "To join this lot of crazy motherfuckers?"

I took a step in his direction. Five soldiers immediately surrounded me at gun-point.

"Only a sick invalid like you could hope of recruiting me!" I stabbed my words like a knife in his chest; I thought I even saw him squirm a little.

The interpreter fell silent in his astonishment without translating my last words.

"Translate that for him!" I snarled out, "Or I'll cripple your other hand!"

He goggled his eyes at me. A gun-mouth knocked me gently from behind. It was my personal favorite – Patton:

"Take it easy, pal!" he scraped. His voice gave away his frantic desire that I would not listen; on the contrary – he wanted me furious, so that he could crush me completely.

"Come on, translate for him!" I ordered the interpreter again.

Though trembling, he obediently did so. Borgia looked at me gravely and clutched his teeth.

"Please," Patton chipped in from behind, "do something."

The lights flickered. It was about time!

"Remember what you were going to say," I said to Borgia, "and you'll tell me later."

I turned to Patton:

"You want me to do something?" I smiled, "You got it!"

I turned back to Borgia:

"By the way, I have a confession to make. I am sick too. I also suffer a complex. But mine is worse! I also suffer from multiple personality disorder and keep pretending to be something I'm not. You see," I grinned happily, "I keep pretending I'm a good and nice man."

He puckered his brows in surprise.

"You have no idea how hard it is for me sometimes!" I went on "I just want to be myself and feel good!" I grinned again. "And I also want to point out that I have absolutely no imagination! And since I bear an insatiable hatred for all of you, I don't see what else is there to be done, except to kill you all!"

I bent at lightning speed, and in the same time I grabbed the gun mouth of the guard standing in front of me. The rest of the guards were shooting somewhere above my head. I pushed hard the guard with my left hand and turned him to the rest of the shooters. He staggered and dropped the shotgun. I threw myself on the floor and stroke down the five guards. Then I rolled on the side and stood on one knee next to Borgia's chair. Everyone was aiming at me.

"Come on, shoot your boss!" I shouted.

I could feel the hatred. I aimed the gun at Borgia's head. In the same time, I grabbed the back of his wheel-chair.

"We're going for a walk."

I pushed the chair back to the other door. There were only three armed guards there. Although I seemed an easy target, they didn't dare to shoot; they were afraid they might hit their master. I kept pushing the chair, looking in all directions to see of the guards were planning to do something. The tension in the air was growing thicker; I could feel it and I expected someone to lose it and start shooting. Some of hoses unplugged from the pushing and Borgia moaned. The High Council jumped in their seats, but could do nothing.

"Stop!" Hans Zimmer cried out. "You're going to kill him!"

I halted and looked the three at the door. Then I turned to Zimmer and replied coldly:

"Yes, that's a definite possibility!"

I lifted the shotgun and cut down the three at the near door. They didn't even have the time to react. Swearing burst among the guards in the other end of the hall. I turned to Zimmer again:

'Now it's your turn.'

I jumped at the light switch, pressed it and immediately jumped aside, rolled on the floor and waited. I saw the lights of the shots and heard the reports – they were piercing the wall around the door.

It was time to do my trick.

I stood up and raised my hands high in the air, spread at a 45º angle. You remember the two rings – the gift from my two lovers, right? Well, I lied about it. Victor Dalloway gave them to me. As a symbol of true love and devotion. I closed my eyes and pressed two small grooves on them. Some microscopic mechanisms threw out some small shots, which ignited and quickly burned out with blinding brightness. I'm not sure if it was magnesium or something else. But it was blinding1

Now, imagine a dark room where everyone is looking at you with eyes wide open and intense. The effect resembles a kick in the balls…well, in the eyes in our case. It goes straight into the brain!

No one in this room, except me, would be able to see or think straight for more than ten minutes.

I opened my eyes slowly. The guards had switched on the lights on their weapons. These lights were circling the room chaotically. The people were blinded. I went and switched the lamps on. The armed men were looking around helplessly, reaching out with their left hands. They were holding their guns in their right arms, but didn't dare to use them – they might shoot each other. Stepping light as a feather, I collected their weapons. I treated everyone alike – I went to them, punched them in the throats and took away their pieces. There weren't much left – about fifteen or so. It took me three or four minutes to disarm them. They didn't resist at all. They were like chicken, totally blind in the dark – you could do whatever you like with them. I pushed them to the middle f the room by the table and Giuseppe Borgia's chair. They were standing blind, quiet and totally helpless. Alistair Conroy and carter Dell were suffering the same. Dalloway and I decided not to tell them about the rings, because they might have blown it.

After that I looked at Borgia. The son of a bitch was able to see perfectly! Obviously he had felt the trick coming and had closed his eyes on time. At least he was breathing with difficulty. He was in his death throes. I glanced at the hose for his breathing set – I had unplugged it while I was pushing the chair. I grabbed the hose and examined the equipment.

The door in the opposite end of the room opened. I lifted my shotgun. It was Victor, dressed as a guard. He smiled friendly. I lowered the weapon and examined the machine again. I finally saw the O2 sign and plugged the hose in.

Giuseppe Borgia started sucking the air in and mumbled behind his mask:

'Grazie!'

'Are you planning to kill him, 'Dalloway wanted to know, 'or marry him?'

'I just want him to remain conscious!' I replied coldly. 'Did you manage to do it?'

'It was a bit hard, but yes, I did. I think if we press that button, this shed will collapse…'

'Are you ready for this?' I looked at him with all seriousness.

'Meaning?'

'There are women and children across the hall.' I replied 'Will you be able to sleep well afterwards?'

'My dear, 'he said with unexpected firmness, 'What do you think my job with these brats was so far?'

I glanced at the "brats". They were standing together like helpless chicken without their mother hen. They only had to cheep to make the picture perfect. More precisely, they didn't dare to utter a word. The High Council members were sitting at their seats, also blind and helpless.

I said to Conroy and Dell:

'Stay put, I'll lead you out in a second.'

'What's going on?' Hans Zimmer asked furtively.

'You gave us away and sentenced us to death.' I replied 'Now there's a small change of plan. Now we are giving you away. Hey, interpreter!' I cried out 'I want you to translate something to your master.'

The youth was still squatting like a trained dog, although his master's chair was long gone. Staring blankly, he turned to me ad asked furtively:

'What are you planning to do?'

'Just translate!' I ticked him off 'Borgia, my man, listen now, I want to ask you something.'

The young man translated and the Borgia nodded.

'Has it ever occurred to you to ask yourself how all the people you killed felt in their moments of death? Have you ever asked yourself if it hurt or if they felt despair, terror and abandonment?'

'No!' he answered firmly 'I didn't care about that!'

That was what I thought. I nodded:

'Yeah, sure. Let me ask you something else. The people in the ballroom – they are all your faithful watchdogs, right? I mean, they are either on your pay roll, or your partners, or your parasites, right?'

'Yes,' he nodded.

I also nodded to myself.

I came nearer and knelt in front of his chair. A big mistake – I almost paid with my life for it! People say: kill your enemy, don't hug them.

'I want to tell you that I really respect you. 'I said seriously 'As a warrior, you're one in a thousand! I even like you/ but if I let you live, you will never stop before you finish me off, right?'

He waited for me translation and then nodded affirmatively.

'So, you see, I can't let you live!' I finished and was about to stand up. In that same moment he reached his right hand and grabbed me by the throat in an iron claw. I tried to open his fingers with both of my hands but to no avail. It was as if a demon was squeezing the life out of me! Dalloway ran and wanted to interfere. I looked him so fiercely, that he startled and stopped. But I was starting to lose my strength. The son of a bitch was cutting the blood flow to my brain. My vision was blurring.

And then I met his eyes.

His eyes were radiating great power! Cruelty and fierceness. He would stop squeezing my throat one or two hours after I was dead. But I also saw something else. A feeling of superiority. Mockery. Pure mockery! He, the handicapped half-dead cripple who needs a machine to keep him alive was about to kill me – the healthy and strong!

That mockery helped me gather my strength back. I stood up abruptly and stepped back. He didn't let go; he was hanging on my neck. He tried to grab me by the balls with his left hand. I flew into a rage! I took two of his fingers and twisted them backwards until they cracked really loud. Then I hit him four times in his head with my elbow. I weakened him and he let go. He dragged down to my feet. I took some breath loudly and stepped back. He was going to smother me, that stupid son of a bitch! Single-handedly!

I looked down to him. He was pulling himself together and was looking at me viciously. I kicked him in the diaphragm. As I grabbed him by the lapels of his expensive suit, I lifted him up and threw him back in his chair:

'Go back to your cripple chair!'

I didn't need to explain, the boy obediently translated everything. Borgia was looking at me like a lion in a cage. With wheezing and gurgling, barely breathing, he still managed to utter something. The interpreter did his job:

'I am in a wheel-chair, but you are not a match for me! You'll never accomplish even one hundredth, one thousandth of what I have accomplished! People will never know who you were! And I am part of the History!'

'You're right.' I replied 'You are about to become history!'

I looked at Dalloway:

'Are we going?'

He nodded. We took Conroy and Dell by the hands and headed for the door.

'Hey, what's going on?' Zimmer shouted as he heard us opening the door.

'We've placed bombs all over the castle.' Dalloway was very serious and business-like. 'We are activating them in a minute and burry you here.'

'You can't do that!' the spokesman cried out. 'We are all here, how can you do that to us?'

'That's easy.' I answered.

'But we all have children!' another member shouted.

'Think about all the parents you've killed.' I scolded him.

'That's not normal!' a third guy chipped in 'You are planning to murder us, without even giving us a chance to defend ourselves!'

'Yes. 'I answered coldly 'Just as you did all along.'

'But that's not fair, 'a fourth one cried 'We don't see anything! You'll slaughter us like animals! What kind of people are you?'

'You're all just a large Tumor!' I shrugged 'And we are the Surgeons!'

I opened the door. An armed guard was holding Elizabeth by the hand. I was holding Conroy. Both the guard and Elizabeth were startled. I took advantage of that and kicked the guard's chin really hard. Sometimes my feet are really fast. He fell unconscious. She was dumbfounded.

'I'll ask you only once,' I told her gravely 'do you have anything to do with this Organization or you are with them by coincidence?'

She gapped.

'Answer me!' I growled.

'They said you wanted to see me. 'She started all confused 'What organization…?'

'Come with us!' I demanded.

'Are you sure about this?' Dalloway asked.

'What's going on?' Elizabeth asked.

'No, I'm not.' I answered Dalloway.

I took Elizabeth by the elbow and dragged her along. Conroy was leaning on my other arm and kept quiet. That was even better.

End 1 -
A Happy One

We entered the ball-room. Two armed men, two blind men and one dumbfounded woman. The rich hypocrites there were still playing Lords and ladies. There was pleasant music in the air and about fifty or sixty dancing couples. Some of the masked people were gathered around the pool tables in one of the corners – about twenty men and women. The other corner of the hall was transformed into a playground for the children with all sorts of climbers and slides. Two infant girls were grabbing each other's hair and trying to bite each other. As Borgia would have said, *"That's Life, there's nothing more to it."* The rest of the guests, probably more than a hundred, were sitting in sofas and armchairs near the tables and talking. Were they discussing the weather? Or the starving children of Somalia?

They still had their masks on. That's the hypocrisy of the powerful for you! They wouldn't show their faces even to each other, because they were afraid one of their own might screw them up!

I fell nauseated.

All of a sudden an old acquaintance stood before my eyes – The prisoner priest. He saw me and gapped with astonishment:

"What are you doing here, my son?"

"I'm just passing. What are *you* doing here?" I exclaimed.

"I'm trying to save a soul or two." He looked around "but that's nearly impossible!" he shook his head with grief. "They are so pleased with their lie, wickedness and evil-doing! All my efforts come to no avail!" he shook his head again.

I asked him, "Don't you want to help the rest of the world a little?"

He puckered his brows:

"What do you mean?"

"To purge the World from all that wickedness?"

"I don't understand." He shook his head.

"The entire castle is mined," I explained "we're going to blow it up in a minute."

"You're going to kill all these people just like that?" Elizabeth exclaimed.

"I won't even bat an eyelid!" I answered.

"But there are children here!" she exclaimed indignantly "Are you going to kill them too?"

"They are little snakes, just like their parents." I snarled out. "Give them five or six years more and they'll start killing, plundering and raping! Then I'd like to hear what you think about it!"

I was about to continue my way, when the Priest reached out and put his palm on my chest. He looked at me firmly and accusingly. But there was something else in his eyes – such depth and comprehensiveness that I fell weak in the knees!

"Who are you to play God?"

His voice was like an avalanche. The words were ringing in my head.

I dropped my eyes.

He was right! Who am I to decide the life and death of these people! It didn't matter there were women and children there. I just didn't know them in person; I didn't know what kind of people they were! I had no right to kill them without knowing them in person. Even if they were thieves and murderers! All of them! I didn't know them and I had no right to do it! And even if I knew them, who am I to decide their fate?

There were too many freaks and monsters walking freely in the world! Two hundred more or less... what difference did it make?

I looked at Dalloway:

"Let's kick them out!"

He nodded. Both, I mean the fourth of us, if you count Elizabeth and the Priest, were shouting as loud as we could:

"There's a bomb in the castle! Leave immediately! There's a bomb in the castle!"

And since everyone was just staring blankly at us, we opened fire at the ceiling. Only then people started to move. The women and the kids were screaming, the men were shouting to hurry.

It was interesting to see how two hundred people would vanish in five minutes! It resembled an illusionist's trick! We poked them from behind like the shepherd drives the herd.

We left the castle and ran across the meadow twenty yards away from it. We were reaching the first line of trees from the park. The people had removed their masks. There were no freakish faces underneath, but normal frightened ones. Pity! I would've liked it better if I saw the villains had demonic features. It would have been easier to understand; now I had to face the fact that the thieves, murderers and marauders are just like everybody else – regular people!

"Let's see what you've done." I said to Dalloway.

He smiled and took out a remote:

"I did something all right."

He activated the equipment and pressed another button. Ten seconds of nothing followed. I looked at him inquisitively. He shrugged.

Then the explosions began. One after the other – more than fifty. In the beginning the castle remained unharmed, as if the blasts were not meant for it. But after the tenth explosion it started to shake. After the twentieth one of its sides collapsed. We were all pressing our ears – the blasts were deafening! Each of them punched us in the stomach. After the last blow, as if by command, the entire huge building collapsed in rumble and dust. A few bulky stone blocks tumbled down in our direction and stopped ten feet away from us. It was… impressive!

A gigantic cloud of dust and smoke remained where the castle used to be and was now spreading all around.

"Good job!" I praised Dalloway.

"What just happened?" asked Carter Dell.

"We just fired Giuseppe Borgia and the High Council." replied Victor.

"I can't believe you did it!" he exclaimed, while something resembling a smile appeared on his face.

I looked around. The people, who were enjoying their fancy-dress ball just a minute ago, were now running wildly to their cars; some of them were carrying their children.

"Their conscience can't be squeaky clean, if they're running away like that." Victor noted profoundly.

"Does that mean that there is no more Organization?" asked Conroy, still blinded and doubtful.

"The High Council is no more." I corrected him.

"This is the same thing." Carter Dell straightened me.

"If you say so." I shrugged.

"Will someone please explain to me what's going on?" Elizabeth asked finally.

"We just carved out a tumor." answered Dalloway.

"We cut a monster's head." Carter Dell explained.

"We seized the existence of a very bad Organization." nodded Alistair Conroy.

She looked at me. I shrugged:

"We killed a few dozens of villains." I said truthfully.

"Now what?" the Priest asked.

I looked around. The explosion had died down. The huge dust cloud over the former castle would blow over … soon. The air was just… lovely! The meadow looked so much better with the castle hanging over it!

The forest was better off without the castle.

The world was better off without the castle.

"Now," I looked at the Priest, "now I am starting anew."

I looked at Elizabeth;

"Can I count on you that you never saw me here?"

She fell silent for a while, staring at me with a bouquet of feelings in her eyes. Then she nodded.

"Well," I looked at each of them, "let's get in the car and go home."

We crossed the park and headed for the parking lot.

The night was really splendid!

Where would we go next? What were we to do?

Well, only God knows such things…

The important thing was that we survived. And maybe, just maybe, we won a peaceful future for ourselves…

Bullshit! It's all crap and bullshit!

We learned that the nasty brats and bitches are everywhere, and especially on the high places of power. And if you want to have a good free life, you have to lock them in their fucking castle, blind them and then blow them up!

Then you leave breathing deeply the fresh fragrant night air.

That's all.

I wish you all the best.

End 2 - Not A Great One

We entered the ball-room. Two armed men, two blind men and one dumbfounded woman. The rich hypocrites there were still playing Lords and Ladies. There was pleasant music in the air and about fifty or sixty dancing couples. Twenty of the masked men and women were playing pool in the near right corner. The far right corner of the hall was transformed into a playground for the children with all sorts of swings, climbers and slides. Two infant girls were grabbing each other's hair and trying to bite one another.

Here was a makeshift theatrical stage to the left, with chairs placed in a semicircle. All chairs were occupied by people with glasses in their hands. The following performance was going on at the moment:

A road policeman had stopped a BMW for speeding. The driver was clearly under the influence. He was driving his… girlfriend. All roles were performed by children, not more than 9-10 years old.

"Do you know how much over the limit you were driving?" the "road cop" asked harshly.

"Urrrgh…officer…" the driver was slightly lisping and his legs were shaky, "it couldn't have been…so much, huh?"

"You were driving with 137 miles per hour!" the officer of the law raised his voice "at maximum allowed speed of 80! And you're drunk on top of everything!" he sounded quite natural.

He was a good actor and was worth of applauses the parental audience gave him. The fathers enthusiastically were raising their glasses, while the mothers were chain-smoking.

"Okey-dokey, mister policeman," the driver said with appease, "can we do something about it…"

"Do what?" the officer was really pissed off. "I'm giving you a ticket and from then on it's up to the chief!"

"Why… officer," the drunken mistress interfered, barely standing on her feet, "let me give a blowjob and let's just forget about it, okay?"

"I beg your pardon?" the cop looked at her reproachfully, "How old are you?"

"Don't count my years, count my clients!" she answered.

The male audience roared in approval as one, and the women smiled faintly, looked at each other with understanding and smoked their cigarettes.

"Get in, you stupid whore!" her "boyfriend" roared beastly.

She shrugged, sucked n invisible cigarette, shook her bootie and with grace and dignity sat in the car. There was another round of applause.

"Believe me, two years from now I am all over her, no matter if they'd pit in jail for it!" one of the men shouted; his neighbors neighed in ecstasy and his wife just smiled faintly.

The jealous boyfriend turned to the cop:

"Please, chief, let's leave it at that! Here's five hundred…"

"I beg your pardon?" the cop cried out indignantly.

"Okay, then, here's a grand…"

"What do you think you're doing?"

"All righty, tell me how much you want?"

The cop looked down and thought about it. Then he looked at him with brightened eyes:

"I know you're in the drug and hooker business. I want in. my cousin works at the customs and…"

He couldn't go on. The driver took out "a gun" and shot him point-blank in the head. The cop fell down. The driver shouted at his girlfriend:

"Come here, you cow! Grab him by the legs! We'll burry him somewhere. Jesus, that's five today! To hell with these greedy bastards!"

"Well," she shrugged, "I offered him a blowjob and the stupid son of a bitch refused…"

"Shut the fuck up!" the jealous guy scolded her.

"It was okay for me, if he wanted to fuck me in the ass," she added and looked down coyly, "only for your sake, babe!"

He didn't say a word. He just went and grabbed her, placed her on the hood on her stomach, took off her panties and "fucked" her hard. Then the two put the body in the trunk and set off.

The sketch was crowned with roaring applause by the audience. The actors were called for an encore three times!

I decided it was time to leave. I poked my companions:

"Come on!"

"And these were children?" Elizabeth couldn't believe her eyes.

"Yeah." Conroy answered, not really believing it himself.

"Oh, you can see?" I was glad.

"I prefer I didn't." he shook his head.

"Truth hurts." Dalloway announced facetiously, "It is really going to hurt from 'Our Truth' in a sec!"

"Pardon?" Elizabeth didn't get it.

"The castle is mined." I replied while I was dragging her along. "We are about to blow it!"

"You're going to kill all these people just like that?" she exclaimed in disbelief, "I don't believe it! You're not that kind of person!"

"Okay, then," I nodded, "just watch."

"You can't kill them!" she cried out, "There are children here!"

"In five years' time the little snakes will be worse than their parents!" I snarled out. "Then I'd like to hear what you think about it!"

"But you can't just…they are little children!"

"I won't even bat an eyelid!" I answered.

I grabbed her by the elbow to prevent her from doing something stupid. We passed among the dancing couples undisturbed. We passed by the kids' corner. One of the girls had finally managed to bite the other on the nose and was now playing happily with her newly-conquered toy. The bitten one was sitting, crying her eyes out. She was holding her nose, which was bleeding profusely and the blood was dripping on the floor and on her dress. Her parents were… somewhere…

We left the castle and walked some twenty feet away from it. Dalloway took out a remote and turned it on.

"Are you really going to do this?" Elizabeth said quietly, "And why?"

"Because everyone inside is so wicked they don't deserve to live!" I roared with hatred.

I glanced at Dalloway. He pressed a button. Nothing happened for a few seconds. He shrugged.

"You're useless!" I scolded him.

Then the explosions began. There were fifty or so. They started from the back and spread to the side walls and into the main entrance. After the tenth explosion the castle started to shake. The enormous building collapsed within itself with fiendish rumble and waves of dust. We were all pressing our ears; nevertheless, we were deafened for a moment. A couple of bulky stone blocks tumbled down in our direction and stopped a few feet away from us. The rumble went on. The mountain of dust was spreading around.

I think Elizabeth was screaming.

Victor Dalloway was grinning at the destruction he caused… hmm… that was slightly insane.

Carter Dell and Alistair Conroy were staring in disbelief. Maybe they thought they still couldn't see and now they were dreaming?

It's okay. They will believe it. I hope they'll start a normal life.

And what about me?

I looked at Elizabeth. She was crying. What can one do – sometimes it is necessary for gentle creatures like her to witness the bad side of this lousy life. I wished that would happen as rare as possible. Or wouldn't have to happen at all. I wished life was better…

I told her "You're so beautiful!"

She looked at me startled. She was simply irresistible with all the tears and smeared make-up!

"You are a murderer!" she pointed her finger at me with accusation. "You are a monster!"

"Not anymore." I shook my head, "It's over!"

She kept staring at me, with a bouquet of feelings in her eyes.

"Would you like to do somewhere?" I asked.

She stared at me for about a minute, then came near and laid her head on my chest.

"Take me away from all this dirt and death." she sobbed.

How could I refuse?

Oh, yes. Without as much as the quiver of an eyelid.

Did I refuse her?

I hold her in my arms and looked at Dalloway:

"Glad to have known you!"

"C'mon! Get the hell out of here!" he grinned happily.

Then I looked at Dell and Conroy:

"Gentlemen."

They nodded solemnly. I winked at Victor. Elizabeth and I headed for the car in the parking lot.

Well…

We'll see…

Maybe it will all work out…

The future will tell…

In any case, the girl is a sweetie and we won't get bored.

Did I mention that just as we were getting in the car, Elizabeth took out a gun from somewhere and pointed it straight into my head? She accompanied all that with a dead serious look and the kindest command:

"Don't move or I'll blow your brains out, I mean it!"

"You…?" I was about to say something.

I heard the police sirens surrounding me. I stopped.

Everything around, even the air I thought, was crowded with police cars and some vans without any markings or license plates. Armed and hooded men jumped out of them. They surrounded the car and made it clear how serious they were.

For a moment, for one very long moment I wanted to take the gun from Elizabeth's hand (it was close at hand and it would have been over in just a few seconds) but then I gave up the idea. I don't know why.

So, they arrested me again.

They didn't sentence me to death this time.

Apparently, because I had "helped neutralize a dangerous international criminal organization."

Otherwise…

I am again in "The Holy Trinity".

Again I work on my favorite dummy.

Again I got acquainted with some new inmates who wanted me. Nice fellas…

Again I see a shrink two times a week…

Again it's Elizabeth…

Hmm…

Well…

I like it!

She always frowns and treats me with bitter coldness like she's out of reach.

Hmm…

I think something good may come out of this one…

And End 3 –
The Ugly Version

"Every man dies. Not every man really lives."

— William Wallace

We left Dalloway by the car with the explosives and continued merrily our way. Carter Dell was driving. The rest of us were checking the perimeter.

A couple of miles away from the castle we came across a barrier with sentinels. They stopped us and examined us carefully. They called on the radio. Asked us where "our fourth one" was. I told them he had been getting on my nerves, so I "had left him somewhere along the road." They called on the radio again. Then nodded assent and let us through.

So far, so good.

A mile away we stopped at another barrier with sentinel. They repeated the procedure. They let us through. At that exact moment, the Vision overwhelmed me again. I saw Hans Zimmer flying this way, heading a pack of hungry helicopters, full of a few companies of well-trained, unscrupulous assassins. Big shunt neon letters were decorating his forehead – they read that he wanted me really bad, better alive than dead, so that he could torture me a little bit before he sends me to the afterlife with the proper receipt.

"Stop!" I ordered Carter Dell.

"But –" he was about to say something.

"I said, stop!" I snarled out.

The sentinels were way behind us. We pulled over behind a turn, among the huge trees in the park. I explained them both with simple words:

"Things are starting to look nasty! Our babe Hans Zimmer is flying over with a bunch of thugs under his command. I think it will be best if you stay here. When it's all over, I'll come and get you, if I'm still alive."

"What do you mean, 'if you're still alive'?" exclaimed Alistair Conroy.

"Haven't you heard," I explained patiently, "that sometimes people die? Maybe it's my turn today."

"How can you speak so calmly and irresponsibly of such things?" carter Dell was openly indignant.

"Just like that!" I ticked him off, "Mom couldn't raise me properly and dad was too good to even try!"

Carter Dell shook his head and Conroy said:

"You're totally insane!"

"Yeah," I nodded "now get lost, I have an important meeting!"

They got off the car in silence. I moved to the driver's seat. I pulled down and the window and told them:

"You better climb up a tree, I'm not messing around. If I don't come back in a couple of hours..." I shut up dramatically.

"What?" Conroy asked.

"Buy a gun and shoot each other dead! First the one, then – the other!" I winked and set off.

If I told you I had a plan that would be a big fat lie! I didn't have a plan. I only knew that I have to end it all right here and now. I didn't want to risk the lives of Dell and Conroy – they were too much of nice guys for that kind of job! Now, Dalloway was military and things like that were part of his everyday activities.

A third guard post stopped me. Wow, that was a hell of a park! They examined me so closely, as if they were planning to buy me. They called the radio one more time. I was prepared for their next move.

As they were talking on the radio (actually, only one of the guards was talking), they suddenly aimed their machineguns at me. It was about time! I was getting itchy from all this idleness!

"Turn off the engine!" one of them ordered and came to my window, pointing the gun at my head.

I stared at him with resentment. He put the mouth of the gun through the window and leaned in my temple:

"Do it!"

Just perfect! I love those kind of intimate relationships! I turned off the engine. Then I switched to first gear, twisting my body a little more than it was necessary. The muzzle followed me, still pressed on my temple. But the thing is that when you're focused on following one movement, you lose bits of the big picture. Following my head, the guard didn't see my left arm. I said I twisted a little more than necessary. When I turned to my original position, I twisted my head and body on the left. The muzzle was now slightly aside from my head. The most it could do was to blow a piece of my left ear off and women would stop falling for me. Big deal! As a continuation of that pretty natural movement, my left arm lifted up and grabbed the mouth of the gun shortly after the guard started shooting. I put it aside, and grabbed the left hand of the guard with my right one. I pulled him up with all the strength I could gather, turning him backwards on the right. He hit his head on the car, handed me the gun and fell down. Then it was easy – the other two started shooting ruthlessly at me, which gave me the right to kill them, too. I got off the car. I wondered for a moment if

I should take hostage the "sleeping beauty". I decided to spare his life – "his colleagues" would shoot him without a moment of hesitation. That was why I left him sleeping on the ground.

I hoped Victor was making faster headway than me, or else we were doomed!

I was sure that the shots were heard from the distance and that a pack of uniform predators were running in our direction. I knew that when they saw their fallen comrades, they would feel the long-forgotten team spirit, sympathy unheard of so far, a selfless love and passionate desire to see me down!

I had to be faster, smarter and nastier than them!

I drove the car to the trees and crashed it in the wooden sentinel shed. I came through the window – the impact had twisted the door and sealed it. I took the machineguns of the two guards and tried to blow up the car. If you think it happened right away, you're mistaken. I ran out of bullets in the first gun and threw it on the ground angrily. I tried the second one. I succeeded. It was really nice to watch it blow up and twist in the air!

Filled with exaltation, I slipped in the bushes among the trees. The guards would surely have dogs. I'm not really a dog person. Which way was the castle? I climbed up a tree – I was very good at climbing when I was a little boy. I searched the perimeter. Oh, there it was on the left, five hundred yards away. There was this big woodless space around it, though. It was about a hundred yards; hmm, I would need a guard's uniform. I could see ten guards around. How thoughtful and kind – to bring the uniforms themselves! Should I shoot them from above? No, that's too low!

I got down and sneaked back to the barrier. I wished I could snatch a uniform without having to kill anybody.

Truth be told, I wished none of this ever happened. I wished I never saw the congressmen in the Mercedes that morning!

Nothing that has happened so far, appealed to me!

Would I kill him again, if I saw him doing what he did?

Yes! I would also kill the corrupted cops before they shot the girl!

Would I kill anybody else from this moment on?

Hmm…yes! Whoever, whenever, however, if necessary!

That was how I saw things. I didn't perceive murder as an act of retribution for the evil-doing, but as a precautionary measure against the harm the bastard might do in the future! Never again!

Some of these here didn't understand the harm they were causing; they even thought they were doing the right thing. Did that make them innocent? Do you think if they got some clarification on how wrong they were, they would stop?

That wasn't of my immediate concern.

What actually was of my immediate concern was that they were planning to do some harm and the right thing to do was to stop them quickly and effectively, no explanations necessary!

I didn't summon them here, so I didn't feel responsible!

Enough musing! I needed a uniform.

I sneaked out carefully. I didn't want them to notice me. If they noticed me, I had to kill again. I didn't mind it, but that doesn't mean I liked it.

It was too easy. The group spread out fan-shaped to search for me. They had seen their dead colleagues and the unconscious guy. They also saw the blown up car and that there was no body in it.

I lurked in the bushes. A guy passed quite near me. I waited a bit, so he could pass me by I showed my head to look around. Then I caught up with him in two leaps and hit his carotid from the back. He immediately lost consciousness. I grabbed him, so he wouldn't crash down and make some noise. I started undressing him.

Why didn't I take the clothes of my sleeping beauty at the barrier, you may ask? I didn't want them to suspect I was planning to sneak into the castle in my Sunday clothes, that was why!

And why did I blow up the car?

It's hard to give a straight answer.

In the beginning, I was planning to place inside the body of one of two dead guards and make it look like it was my corpse.

Then I understood two things at once. First, they were hardly that stupid to buy this! Second, and more important to me, that would have been really vicious! To mutilate the corpse of the guy, so that he wouldn't even get a decent burial – Fie! That was not how I did things!

I hate viciousness!

So, why did I blow up the car after all? Maybe out of anger. I was angry at everyone who helped bringing me into this mess!

Dressed as one of the guards, I caught up with my colleagues, searching for me among the trees and in the bushes. I doubted they could see my wicked face in the dark. The only thing they saw was my uniform. I was planning to enter the castle as one of them – that was the kind of unscrupulous skink I was!

I really hoped it would work. And fast, because Little Hans was storming here and was in a really bad mood.

We searched through the trees for a while, and then I think the commander got orders to retreat. They lined up. The commander was calling us individually by name and everyone responded. What now? Right, I saw the name 'McCormack' written on my left jacket pocket.

"McCormack?" the commander cried out.

"Here!" I roared back in a strong macho voice.

So far, so good. "To buy a pig in a poke," a wise man had once said. Was it D'Artagnan? But when we show up in the light, they will call my bluff really fast and my ass would have too many visitors in one go! We were heading back. We passed by the barrier where I blew up the car. Very well! We passed it by. We weren't walking in line any more. I slowed down little by little. After a while I was all alone. I stood still, then knelt in the bushes. The others were walking ahead. They wouldn't do another check-up before they reached the castle. I returned to the barrier, which now had welcomed three new sentinels, guarding the burning car. The dead bodies and the unconscious guy were taken to the castle by the soldiers in front.

"They sent me to replace you and sent you back to the caste!" I commanded.

"Why?" one of them asked.

"Why didn't they call us on the radio?" the second one asked too.

"That son of a bitch was spotted entering the castle and they need more people on the premises!" I replied.

"Come on, then." The first one said and left.

"And you will stay here?" the second guard asked.

"That's tight." I nodded.

"Okay, then." He left as well.

Sometimes I really love military men! By strenuous exercise they were able to achieve the murderous art of not thinking. Murderous for them, that is.

"Wait a minute," the third one said and lit up my face.

Sometimes thinking is also deadly. This guy blew my cover. I kicked him in the chin, while he was examining my face. The two, who just left, halted and turned around. I didn't wait for them to see my face. I leaped between them. With the end of my left palm I hit the throat of the guy standing on my left. With my right fist I punched the other between the eyes. They murmured something unhappily, then knelt down and after a short period of brainstorming, lay on the ground.

Good. I checked my machine-gun, and then grabbed some ammunition from the lying guards.

It was time to enter the castle – I had a lot of work down there.

I wondered what Victor was doing. He was a fine man, he would manage!

The uniform consisted of trousers, a jacket and a cap, very convenient if you want to hide from the cameras.

I left in high spirits, with a slow pace, no hurry. The castle was waiting for me and wasn't going anywhere.

You probably think I had some great master plan, some exquisite strategy or some genius thought?

I have to disappoint you – I didn't hold anything up my sleeve. I am no strategist or tactician; I'm not a great thinker either. I've never taken castles by storm before. I am new to this craft. I may never perfect it.

But I know one thing, if you catch your enemy by surprise, there is always this moment of being startled and if you're determined, quick and precise, you can kill them. How can one surprise their enemies the most? Well, by doing what they least expect of you.

I brazenly headed for the main entrance. With my stolen uniform, cap and machine-gun on my shoulder. It was… despicably impudent! My specialty.

I reached the large meadow by the castle. I heard some music. There were some couples engaged in sexual activities here and there. They were leaning on the trees. Bless them! Both the trees and the people. Generally, when everything else is in order, people only think of sex and nothing else. Nothing new or surprising there.

I came across the meadow to the main entrance, which got bigger and bigger as I approached. It was simply huge! Two guards in uniforms just like mine were standing there. I was planning to nod and come in. When I came nearer, one of them snapped:

"Where do you think you're going?"

My right index finger moaned in a passionate desire to hug the trigger and talk of love for an hour or two. I shushed it to keep quiet and answered the guard:

"I need some coffee!"

"Are you insane?" the other guard exclaimed, "If you enter through here, they'll kill us! The guests are not supposed to see us at all! Go through the other door!" and he showed somewhere on the left.

I nodded as I headed to the appointed direction. I walked around the left side of the castle, checking it carefully. It was pretty huge! It was at least 30 yards tall and had at least two floors. I liked the large stone blocks which constituted the outer wall. The meadow around it was also large – more than 50 yards in diameter. And then there was the gigantic park around the castle! Hmm...Sometimes even I fell for the grandeur but that was just too much!

I saw a small side entrance ahead of me, obviously made way after the whole castle was built. There was a wooden sentry-box, resembling a telephone booth, next to it. Two armed guards were standing nearby, smoking and chatting. A third one was walking around.

All of a sudden, my Vision rang clearly in my head, *'Don't go there! Go round!'*

Crazy, huh? Well, I never followed the common law and I always trust my visions.

I slowed down because I needed time to think. Apparently I had to change my frontal attack with something else.

Right, I got it!

As I approached the sentry, I suddenly turned right to the trees and opened fire. I started swearing in the same time.

The two guards dashed at me. The third one stayed at the sentry-box.

"What the fuck is going on?" the first to arrive asked.

"I saw the bastard; he's hiding behind a tree!" I replied in exaltation.

"Where?" the second guard was looking at the park.

"I saw him right there!" I pointed at nothing in particular, then aimed again, "You, stupid son of a bitch!" I opened fire again.

The two guards also opened fire in the appointed direction. I couldn't hold it anymore, so I dashed to the trees, shouting and firing. The two followed me; I saw them over my shoulder. We entered the tree-line with the bushes and halted. I was listening and looking around with alert, and then decided to go deeper.

"Hey," one of guards whispered behind me, "let's wait for the back-up. It's going to arrive any minute."

"Fuck the back-up!" I replied, "I'll kill him myself!"

I was going deeper and deeper among the trees and bushes. It was dark in there.

"Hey, man, wait!" the second guard whispered "There's our guys!"

It was true – thirty or forty armed men were running out of the castle and into the woods. I had to go.

"Here he is!" I shouted, aimed and opened fire, and then dashed in the woods.

The two guards stood still. They were waiting for their colleagues. Good. I ran a little more into the woods, then slowed down and made a wide semicircle, which led me back, leaving the hit squad somewhere aside.

There were now four guards by the sentry-box.

That plan was long gone.

I turned round and headed for the back of the castle. The wall was made of large hewn stone blocks. Well, I'd better start climbing. I haven't done it in a long time and since my last try I'd put some wait, but it was okay– I could manage. I put the machinegun on my back, rubbed my hands and fingers and cracked all my joints.

Okay, then, if my frontal attack didn't succeed, I would use cunning wickedness and enter their rear.

I started climbing. By the way, I thought at first there might have been cameras on some of the trees, but decided to try my luck anyway. It was surprisingly easy. Look at that – I was so cool and hip! Somewhere in the middle I thought whether sports climbing could be my calling, if it would help me find my place in the world and achieve world recognition, fame, peace of mind and harmony within. The thought was caressing my mind for a whole ten seconds. Then I continued climbing without thinking. I would think about my future after I was done here. If I was still alive to think about it.

I heard the sound of helicopters. Little Hans had arrived! Wasn't it great to have them all in one place? I hope Victor would do his part, too!

Here was the upper edge of the wall. It had embrasures, of course! I peeked through. The castles' roof contained a helicopter landing pad. And some helicopters were landing there just now. Actually, two of them were landing and the rest, ten or so, were just flying around the castle. There were twenty armed men on the roof observing the helicopters. That was really convenient for me! Hans Zimmer and Elizabeth got out of one of the helicopters. That bitch!

Some suits got out of the other helicopter. They had a bad aura. Good, I like bad auras, it frees my inhibitions.

Ten people in total got off the helicopters. I seized the opportunity and leaped over the embrasure to the roof. As I said, the guards were busy with the delegation. I just stepped forward and became one of the guards watching the arrivals. Simple and effective.

They headed for the opposite wall to a tower which was probably leading down to the castle. The chief of the guards called us with a single gesture. We ran up to him and lined up. I was on the right end. He stood before us and shouted:

"In the next 24 hours you won't sleep or rest! I want you to be alert all the time and be sharp! Is it clear?"

"Sir, yes, sir!" everyone roared; I just opened my mouth, because I didn't know the appropriate response.

"Four of you shall remain here, the others – after me!" he commanded again.

I was lucky I wasn't part of the remaining four – they were standing on the left end of the line. We followed the chief in military formation.

Things were starting to look up – the hosts turned out to be polite and invited me in.

We entered the tower and were going down on these narrow winding steps. They were so narrow that two people couldn't walk side by side. We reached the upper floor and entered a hallway through a door. The chief pointed at the first four men behind him and they remained on the floor. The rest of us continued our way down. I slowed down – I wanted to be in the back, so I could reach the first floor. The chief left four more on the next floor. They dashed across the hallway just like diligent boy scouts. Two on the left and two on the right.

Actually, one remained by the stairs next to the door. Probably each floor was framed by a hallway, leading to the various rooms. Was there such a staircase in each corner of the castle? I don't remember seeing four towers, but it sounded logical. The last eight people went down to the first floor. We could hear some loud music. We went across a room with resting sentry. They jumped out of the beds and saluted the chief.

"Run to the park and I want you making rounds 24/7 without stopping!" he said harshly, "Every two hours two of you can come into the castle for coffee and a cigarette, or to the bathroom. Otherwise, no stopping whatsoever!"

"Sir, yes, sir!" they all replied as one, tightened their belts, grabbed the machineguns and flew away.

We went through the other door of the room and stepped on a terrace. The entire first floor was framed by this terrace in its upper end. There was a huge, even gigantic, ball-room underneath. That was where the loud music was coming from. I heard people's voices too.

The chief halted, turned around and announced:

"Your task is to observe and secure, without being noticed! You must not disturb the guests! The same rule of non-stopping applies to you, too! You have the right to have some coffee, a fag and bathroom every hour! Otherwise, you just stand still, observe and if necessary, destroy! I sit clear?"

"Sir, yes, sir!" we roared.

"Shut the fuck up!" he scolded us smiling "Spread along the terrace!"

There were eight of us. We put four in the corners and one in the middle of the terrace, one per each side. I was placed in the middle. The chief nodded with content and left through a door in the terrace end opposite me.

We looked at each other displeased. We were talking 24 hours! Then, as if by an unsaid command, we approached the railings to see what was going on underneath. The hall was really huge, maybe fifty by fifty.

A huge chandelier was hanging from the ceiling – it had at least two hundred lamps and covered some part of the view. However, the room was big enough and there was plenty to see. Sofas were lined up b the walls and next to them – tables with various meals and drinks. The people were wearing old-fashioned costumes, dominoes and masks. Children were running around the tables and the sofas. They were also dressed in old time costumes and wearing masks. That seemed so grotesque to me.

The center of the ball-room was empty. Obviously, they were waiting for the dances later on. Servants were going about the tables with plates in their hands and also wearing fancy dresses and masks. I started to get really irritated.

Pleasant music was filling the air. Something smooth for queens and fags. Splendid!

Actually, after I kill these twelve members of the High Council, I could sit with Victor and wine and dine at the tables of the powerful ones… and we would decide together if we were going to let any of these masked powerful people live.

I was wondering what Victor was doing.

And what was I doing here, dressed as a clown and playing Peeping Tom? And where is my right hand?

I'd better go and do something useful!

I traced the chief's steps. My nearest "colleague" exclaimed:

"Where the hell are you going?"

"I need to take a piss." I replied politely.

"The chief said every hour, and there are hardly five minutes passed!"

"Okay, then," I shrugged "I'm going to help the chief take a piss."

"Don't, there will be trouble!"

I didn't honor him with a response but kept going.

"Freak!" he shouted behind my back.

I get that every day.

By the way, helping the chief take a piss was a great idea! He would surely know where the Council's meetings were held. And he would tell me for sure!

I came through the door I saw him entering. I found myself in a corridor, about ten yards long, ending with a winding staircase, leading up and down. There were doors on both sides. Three on each side of the corridor. I decided to try them one by one. So, the first one on the left – a room with four beds, a wardrobe (it looked like something I just did) and a crooked table. Obviously, that was the sentry room. Well, the sentry was out in the woods. That was very advantageous for me, roaming about the castle. That was a good start. Let's try the first door on the right. Aha! I saw the broad back of the chief. His trousers were loose and down. He was rhythmically rocking forwards and backwards. There was a bed in front of him, but it was empty. I was intrigued! I peeked slightly behind his right shoulder. I see! There was a porn magazine on the bed, and the commander was holding his penis in his hand and doing his thing. The man seemed overwhelmed, so I decided to leave him alone. A guy can go crazy if you interrupt him in the middle of it. Quietly, almost gently I closed the door, folded my arms together and waited. He was picking up speed and slightly moaning. And how strenuous he was! I don't masturbate like that. He beats me on all accounts!

There was a table on the right. He had thrown his uniform jacket on it. A packet of cigarettes was showing from his upper pocket. Perhaps it was curious to see what his master was doing; if it had hands, it would make common cause with his master. I stepped stealthily towards the table, grabbed the packet and took out a cigarette. I put it in my mouth. Would he hear me, if I use my lighter? I doubt it. He won't notice me, even if I slap him on the butt. That's always the case with good hand-jobs. He was completely overwhelmed. I lit up my cigarette and inhaled. Then I retreated to the door and waited. Soon he started pulling it really fast and moaned noisily. A real macho! Why can't a woman see him now, she'll want him immediately, right there and then! He was panting. Brushed off the sweat from his forehead. It was difficult, but worth it. He buttoned up his trousers, then leaned and closed the magazine. I sighed noisily one more time, and turned to the table where his jacket was lying. He didn't see me. Still panting, he reached in his pocket and lit up a cigarette.

And then he saw me.

"Isn't it great to have a hand-job?" I smiled friendly.

He opened his mouth to speak, then remembered he was the commander, and roared instead:

"How long have you been standing there?"

"About ten minutes."

He calculated the time, came to me and said threateningly:

"If you just mention about it to anyone, I'll make you sorry you were ever born!"

"I promise to keep my mouth shut!" I replied.

He fell silent for a while, and then asked:

"What do you want?"

"Take me where the High Council sits."

"Are you out of your mind?" he goggled "We can't even come near that place! Borgia has placed his personal squat of bodyguards. They will kill us no questions asked! They are ferocious butchers!"

"Please!" I begged him with my hands brought together in prayer, "At least tell me where it is!"

"And why do you want to know so badly?" he looked at me extremely suspicious.

"He's sort of my idol, you see!" I said with deep feeling, "Please, at least let me see the guards!" I almost jumped up and down like a child.

He murmured something and looked at me again. I was staring at him with begging eyes. He shook his head, *'What a freak!'* then, he put on his jacket and cap and commanded:

"Follow me!"

"Thank you!" I clasped my hands.

"But you promise you won't mention this to anyone!" he pointed his finger at me.

"I do, I do!" I couldn't stop moving with excitement.

"And you'll do what I say, no matter what!"

"No matter what!" I nodded obediently.

He shook his head again and murmured, "Why do I bother?", then led me on the way.

Well, I can't deny it – I am incredibly lucky! Luck is my bitch! If I see her, I'll buy her one.

I went one floor down. We didn't go through the ball-room. We took a corridor with plenty of doors on the right and none on the left. We reached a winding staircase, leading upwards. We climbed two floors. How secretive! We found ourselves in a corridor, stacked with soldiers. They all had storm-troopers' uniforms and hoods. They must be really ugly without them! They turned to us in an instant; all aiming their pieces, but they saw our uniforms and lowered the weapons. In the other end of the corridor, another newcomer showed up. The procedure with the weapons repeated.

The newcomer headed in our direction. He was an unpleasant man. I mean he had very bad aura. He was dressed on a dark-grey suit. He was mobbing slowly and gracefully, in fact quite casually, like a man who was in total control of the situation and who could do whatever he liked. I was able to see his face as he approached. He was Asian. We stared into each other's eyes; his stare stabbed right in the solar plexus. I felt physical pain in the pit of my stomach and a chill went down my spine.

That was an evil man. A cruel man! I may have imagined this, but I think he smiled at me and nodded. I shivered. He passed the storm-troopers casually, as if they weren't there at all, and went through a door in the middle of the corridor.

So, that was the HQ, good.

And the guy? I had never met such a guy before. I had only heard they existed. The kind that were better never to meet in person.

All right, then; it was going to be one of my worst days, I gathered. I wished I had stayed at home!

What should one do in this situation?

Usually you follow your gut reaction.

I punched the chief with my left hand in the throat. That was easy, because he was standing on my left. He didn't hesitate at all – just fell down quickly and noisily. The troopers stared at me again. I aimed my gun and …saw the Vision. Obviously, it really was one of my critical days. I started shooting them in the faces. It was extremely easy, since the corridor was narrow and they were lining along the walls. Only the nearest two or three soldiers could fire at me, but in the same time they had to expose their backs to the bullets of their colleagues, protecting me with their bullet-proof vests. A simple case of geometry, ladies and gentlemen! That's what happens when you don't think things over. Well, sooner or later, one of the more impatient ones was going to get me, and then what?

There's nothing you can do – life has to end some day. So make the best of it!

The best storm-troopers, for example!

I decided to take them one by one.

I aimed the machine-gun and shot the three nearest soldiers in the faces. That was an ugly sight! Their colleagues behind had already drawn a bead on me I grabbed one of the soldiers I shot by the vest knelt on right knee and used him as a shield. I was shooting, leaning the muzzle on his left shoulder. The blood from his face was dripping on my left shoulder. It was ugly, I tell you. With the kind help of the Vision, I could see clearly and accurately the soldiers presenting immediate danger. And shot them in the faces. The surviving ones were kneeling and lying all behind their dead colleagues. They were professionals. What saved me was the fact that they didn't have gas masks. If they had, they would release some tear-gas and I was history.

Yet, as they say, "Life is perpetual motion." I started moving slowly ahead, dragging, pushing and carrying the dead trooper. I was heading for the door where the nasty guy disappeared. The Headquarters of the Nasty. I was constantly alert if anyone should try to jump me from the back. I was a virgin in that area, after all.

Twice some trooper tried to attack me – such a selfless and stupid thing to do. The Vision was showing the attack a second or two in advance. I had to take him down. Then, another idea came to them. The same idea I showed them in the beginning. They grabbed some of their dead comrades as shields and were sneaking at me. Obviously, they needed some time to overcome the unpleasant feeling that the used the body of one of their own – someone they knew, someone who was just standing there a moment ago. They considered it as an act of perversion, which was perfectly understandable.

Apparently they have never read *"The Volunteers at Shipka"*!

I ran out of bullets, threw away my machine-gun and grabbed another one. I could see the difference right away – this one was bigger and heavier. A military weapon! These guys have gone far in the powerful reach!

Another thought dawned on me. The soldiers were approaching slowly and carefully, but steadily. They were still hiding behind the dead bodies of their comrades.

I halted and placed the gun on my shield's shoulder. I aimed at the hood of a dead body, shielding a trooper and fired. The heavy bullets went through the dead guy's head and hit the living one. He fell on his back, pressed by the weight of the corpse. I did the trick once more, and that was it.

The others had already reached me. They left aside their dead weight, leaped on me and attacked me fiercely.

First I shot one. I greeted with the butt-stock the second soldier in the ankle and then in the chin with a twist. He literally flew back.

The other three aimed at me as one. With a single arched movement of my gun, I pushed aside theirs. They fired and hit the wall. It was such fun! As a continuation of my graceful movement, I hit the attacker standing on the far left on the head. Then, with a butt-stock movement on the right, I hit the right one in the temple. He stepped aside to aim at me. I pushed his gun on the right (his left), and hit his right elbow with the butt. His arm softened. I trooper on the left was also aiming. I knelt down and shot him in the face. After that I returned to my former position. The guy next to me was moving his gun into his left hand. I shook my head and with a kick in the temple, I sent him into oblivion.

It seemed this was it. I looked around just in case. Yes, there were no more troopers. It was so easy!

The HQ was waiting for me. It would have been rude to make them wait any longer. Considering the warm welcome they gave me. I had to show them the feeling was mutual. I took another gun and two spare cartridges, which I tucked in the back of my uniform belt.

I approached the door with alert and pressed the handle with the gun-mouth. I heard massive rhythmic shooting. The door literally smashed into pieces. The opposite wall crumbled from the bullets. I didn't plan it, but I laughed my heart out, just like the village idiot.

I did the restaurant trick again – I peeked through the door frame. Ten muzzles barked fiercely at me.

Why didn't the Vision show that? In the restaurant I could see everything, in all directions. Here the trick didn't work.

So how I am supposed to enter now? Should I do my dead shield trick? No. I looked at a corpse nearby. I took off his bullet-proof vest and put it on. After a moment of hesitation, which lasted an entire second, I put on another one on top. Then I quickly took off some more vests. I went to the door and started throwing the vests into the room. The men inside opened fire. That was exactly what I wanted. I threw the vests in irregular intervals. Every time they thought it was me entering. And every time it was only a vest. After the third one, I heard them reloading. I abruptly threw myself on the ground in front of the door. They looked at me startled. I fired ruthlessly in their faces. They started falling on their backs, still kneeling on their right knees. Only one managed to shot at me, but missed.

I stood up and burst into the room. I reloaded in motion, not checking if there were any bullets in the cartridge.

The Vision showed me ruthless troopers, running to the room. It also showed me that it was really the HQ behind that door. I saw twelve people sitting at a round table in the middle of the room. I saw Alistair Conroy and Carter Dell tied up naked on some metal grates in the opposite left corner of the room. They were unconscious. Shit! I saw dear Hans Zimmer standing by the door, aiming a machine-gun. About ten more people were standing in the same loving position. Aside from the table, in a wheel-chair, sat an old man. That Very Unpleasant Asian was standing right next to him.

I kneeled on one knee and opened fire through the door on Little Hans and his dear friends. They fell down. I ran out of bullets and had to reload. In the meantime, the Vision was showing me how Hans and the others were slowly getting on their feet. Bullet-proof vests!

My father always said that my head was not even a pumpkin, but a gourd, because it never ripens.

I kicked the door open and burst into the room. One of the soldiers pointed his gun at me. I pushed it aside with my muzzle and shot him in the forehead. The Vision was still showing me their movements a second before they actually did them. The picture was still grotesquely blurred, but I was starting to get the hang of it. I was doing well. I shot two more and roared (I was also surprised by the powerful lungs I had):

"Drop your weapons!"

They were wondering whether they should do it. How can they be so dumb? I shot one more. Now they grasped the idea and let go of the pieces.

"Get up and go to the grates!" I commanded.

Slowly and stiffly they started to get up. I flew into a rage:

"Now, stupid!" I roared again and shot one more.

They jumped on their feet and ran to Conroy and Dell. Some guys need a hell of a lot of time to grasp an idea!

I glanced at the High Council. They all had the same suits and haircuts. Dissenters! Zombies!

I looked at the one in the wheel-chair. If the Asian was scary, that guy was really frightening!

There was something like a cabinet on wheels behind him. All sorts of tubules and hoses were coming out of it and penetrating various parts of the old man's body. There were some in his nose, the mouth, in his two elbows. In the trousers in front. In his belly above the belt. Two intravenous sources in his two jugular veins. He was holding an oxygen set in front of his mouth and nose. That cabinet behind him was his life-supporting equipment.

You'll say, what is so scary about this guy? He's just an invalid!

His stare was scary. It had such a frightening power, it made you shiver all over and wish he would never get up from his wheel-chair!

Both the old man and the Asian hadn't moved at all so far. I couldn't see a shadow of fear or tension on their faces. They would never give in and wouldn't stop at nothing. It's better if you never meet such people!

I had a feeling that God created them as an act of boastfulness – see what I can do out of mere albumen!

I approached the High Council table and stared into the eyes of each member. They all had the same expressionless nondescript faces. Puppets with a sense of great self-importance. I wasn't interested.

I glanced at the old man and the Asian. I nodded and they did the same.

"Do we need a translator?" I asked.

"I'll translate for you," the Asian said.

Contrary to his appearance, his voice was soft and lovely. Hmm… that deceitful bastard! I was alert to the best of my abilities.

"What have you done to Dell and Conroy?" I asked the old man.

He waited for the Asian to translate. Then he spoke in Italian and the Asian was translating simultaneously:

"Do you know who I am and where you are?"

"I don't know and I don't care." I responded coldly "I asked you a question."

"My name is Giuseppe Borgia and this is my son Tanaka."

Well, well, so that was Borgia?! I examined him carefully. I have to admit I got the chills again and I felt... sincere admiration! This man was radiating enormous power! Birth, life, misery, pain, joy, grief, love, hatred, violence, and death... The rise and fall of dynasties. Destructive wars. The high and low tides of the world. The World's history!

I had no idea it was possible for one man to gather all that in his gaze and then show it to somebody else!

"You've seen so much!" I told him "You've experienced so many great things!"

He smiled. I cracked my neck and repositioned my machine-gun. I stared coldly at him:

"You've caused too much!"

His smile faded. He spoke and Tanaka translated with his lovely voice:

"I knew you'd come, sooner or later. I didn't know when exactly, but I have waited years for you to come."

I looked at him doubtfully and he continued:

"Everyone convinced me that was impossible and it would never happen. But I knew you existed and you'd come to me. I've been waiting for you!"

What the hell was he talking about?

"How do you think I got here?" he asked "I foresaw and sensed things, events and people; I was ahead of them, so I ruled them."

What?

"I know exactly how you managed to beat Hans Zimmer in the hotel, because I've won many battles in the same way!"

I stared at him.

"Oh, yes," he nodded with a smile "I also have the Vision!"

My legs were shaking. The floor was moving underneath.

"I've warned everyone to expect your arrival, but they didn't believe me," he went on "and here you are at last. I have to admit I'm glad to see you!" he smiled, "I would get up and hold you if I could!"

The red light went on in my head. The shaking was over. I heard a moan from the metal grates. Either Conroy or Dell has regained consciousness and was in pain again.

Electricity went through my body. The hairs on my neck went prickly. I took a good grip of the machine-gun. I gave Borgia a measured nasty smile:

"Good try!"

"You are my twin-brother!" he replied.

Once more the floor was trying to escape under my feet, but I quickly pulled myself together and focused. I smiled:

"You never give up, do you?"

"I don't mean by blood," Borgia shook his head "I mean astral twin brother. You and I are alike!"

Moaning came from the grates. That helped me come to my senses. I saw a warm wave of fury floating in my body. I snarled at the cripple:

"I suddenly remembered I have something more important to do. Do you have anything to say before I finish you off?"

"Come to me!" he let go of the oxygen mask and opened his arms to hug me with all the hanging intravenous systems. "I've been waiting for so long! Together we shall rule the World!"

"I don't feel like it!" I simply said.

I looked at Dell and Conroy. I haven't noticed before they had dark-blue spots, burning marks, and bleeding cuts, maybe from a whip, all over their naked skin.

I felt disgust and frenzy. I looked at Borgia and Tanaka:

"You know what, sometimes I wonder what kind of sick twisted brain the Creator of this leprous world has? I don't understand how he could create so much pain, sickness, suffering and violence? I don't understand how he could create such crooked creatures like men?"

I glanced at Conroy and Dell again. They were both conscious and writhing with pain. They were both dripping blood on the floor.

I turned back to Borgia and Tanaka:

"We can't blame the rapists and the murderers. It's only when they rape and kill, only when they torture their victims and listen to their moans and agony, it's only when they see the pain and suffering on their faces… only then they feel alive! It is the single most vivid experience in their existing. That's what drives them to live on. How can we take that away from them?" I looked at them inquisitively. "God made them that way. Who are we to judge them?"

I shook my head and shrugged:

"On the other hand, some guy comes up now and then and spoils the perfect order in this Perfect World."

I think I grinded my teeth unintentionally:

"It's some nobody like me, coming home from his shift, some butcher," I gave a faint smile. "Actually, when I think about it, this world seems in perfect order. There are predators and herbivorous creatures. The ones devour the others and nothing is wasted. When they die, the plants and the animals become coals which we use for heating… I quite like this World! And here we are – you are twisted sick creatures, and I have nothing to do at the moment, so I'll take advantage of the Creator's Wisdom and entertain myself. I wish you all the best!"

I lifted the machine-gun and…the Vision showed me troopers, coming from my back. I leaped to Borgia, jumped over and stooped behind him. Soldiers burst through the door across the room. I aimed the gun at Borgia's skull. The guys stopped hesitantly.

In that moment I heard someone behind the troopers firing at them. He was very quick and precise, he was using single shots. I took up the same. They started falling one by one.

Dalloway showed up, dressed in a guard's uniform. I shouted:

"I was beginning to miss you!"

He grinned and shot a guy in front of him.

I stood up and lowered the gun. I was about to say something to Dalloway.

I didn't manage to.

Tanaka decided to show me his vicious side.

With unexpected adroitness, fast and precisely he kicked my gun-mouth upwards and then kicked me in the chest, where my heart was. I flew back and slightly in the right. I threw my gun in the air to free my hands and land safely. Obviously, that was what he wanted. I fell on my back and almost immediately he was on top of me, having knives in his hands, god knows where from. I grabbed him by the wrists, and he tried to kick me in the chin. I moved my head aside. He made circular movements with his wrists and cut my both hands. I let go. He pointed a blade in my throat. I protected myself with my left armpit, where he stabbed the knife to the hilt. What an interesting sensation! Sharp pain and then you arm does not belong to you anymore. Tanaka grinned nastily. What a big mistake – he could have finished me off, but he preferred to enjoy his superiority over me. I took advantage and kicked him with a knee in his balls. He moaned in surprise and pain. With an open right palm I whacked him I the face. He tossed back his head. I greeted his chin with my right fist in an old-fashioned way. I think I broke some of his neck bones. Then I pushed him in the chest (I felt unbearable pain in my left hand), threw him aside and stood up. Despite his injuries, he rolled back over his shoulder, kneeled and gave me a vicious look. I had broken his nose. He touched in gently, blew it angrily and wiped it with his sleeve. I glanced at the knife in my left armpit. I took a deep breath and then exhaled. In the same time, I grabbed the haft and pulled it abruptly. Not only did it not come out, but it hurt like hell. Tears appeared in my eyes. Tanaka grinned. I clenched my teeth, grabbed the haft and fiercely pulled out the knife. I couldn't suppress a moan. Tanaka grinned again:

"The little boy wants to play with the big guys!" he showed me his teeth.

I felt dark determination rising within me. I unbuttoned my bullet-proof vests and took them off.

"Hurry up!" standing by the door, Dalloway nervously warned me.

"Shut it!" I replied kindly.

I looked at Tanaka. What I saw was a curled up cobra, ready to strike. I told him:

"I want you to translate something to your father, before I kill you!"

He nodded through clenched teeth. I looked at Borgia. I saw no sign of tension on his face. What a hard stuck-up son of a bitch!

"I only wanted to be left alone." I started "Nothing more! But you insist to show you're better than anyone else at all costs! You want to dominate others forever! You want to decide their fate! To rule the World! To raise and destroy!" I pointed to Del and Conroy, "This is an abomination! You're sick! And there's no cure for your sickness!"

Tanaka was translating between his teeth, barely holding his hatred in. The important thing was that he was translating after all.

"You want me to be a part of all this?" I pointed at the members of the High Council, sitting stiffly as a tableau vivant. "To be a part of all of this madness? Only a sick cripple like you can consider this!" I shook my head.

"You and I are one," he said coldly, "if you don't join me now, you'll do it later! You are on your way to meet me and you will! You know it! And there's no coming back! But then you'll be alone and rejected, just as I am now," his smile could turn blood into ice, "There's no turning back!"

I glanced at Tanaka:

"Are you ready?"

"I'm ready." He nodded.

He stood against me. I have to say, despite his broken nose and the blood on his jacket, he stood proudly and with dignity.

"You've never experienced happiness in your entire lives," I said and he translated to his father without having to ask him, "I am a good and compassionate man. I'll free you from your suffering and the necessity to live."

"You talk too much." Tanaka said between his teeth, "You should've become a public speaker or a writer."

I smiled. He did the same. Then he attacked fiercely. He was moving at incredible speed and my Vision was gone. I had to deal with it by myself.

He attacked me with circular cutting movements to my stomach, chest and throat. Some I deflected, some I left because I considered them to be feints. He attacked me again in the same manner. I sensed a trap and was alert. He attacked again with cutting slashes towards my stomach, chest and throat. Every time in the end of the attack he was leaning forward his right shoulder and his left arm remained behind. I see. When he attacked for the fourth time, there was a knife in his left hand which headed viciously to my loins. I barely deflected it. For just a second, Tanaka leaned forward in his usual manner. I kicked him in the chin he so kindly offered. He softened and stood half-conscious with his legs wide open. I stepped forward and took away the knife from his right hand. I fiercely stabbed it in his neck. His gaze became unfocused, as if he was preparing for the trip to the Other Side. I took away the knife from his left hand, too and turned to his father. I could hear the son falling on the ground behind me.

I didn't have a look – I had more important things to do.

I stood in front of Borgia. He looked at me and spoke, which I didn't expect. Dalloway took up the translation:

"You're going against your nature! Nobody who does that succeeds! I followed my instincts and conquered the World! You won't achieve one thousandth of what I've done! You'll die alone and forgotten, and will become part of the History!"

"You're dead right!" I replied, "You are about to become history."

I stood right in front of him, which I almost had to pay with my life! The cripple took out a knife and stabbed me in the left thigh. I moaned and bent down. Then he grabbed me by the neck with both hands. His grasp was made of steel! I almost lost consciousness. Everything was getting blurred. And then I met his eyes. He looked triumphant and he was smiling. He, the cripple in the wheel-chair, was about to kill me, the young and healthy! Ha-ha-bloody-ha!

I stood up sharply and he hung on my neck. I grabbed him by the waist, lifted him high in the air and smashed him on the edge of the round table, right between two members of the High Council. He let go. Then, he fell on the floor and gave me a nasty look. He hissed something, which Dalloway interpreted:

"You are no match to me!"

"Yeah," I panted, "you're right!"

And gathering all my strength, I stepped on his throat.

I stepped back and looked at Dalloway. He was tense and nervous. He clearly thought we should get the hell out of there.

I pulled out abruptly the knife in my thigh. It hurt terribly and tears appeared in my eyes. I wiped them with my sleeve. No major blood vessels or nerves were harmed. It was bleeding profusely, but there was no serious danger. I took out a handkerchief and dressed the wound straight through my trousers; it didn't have the time to do it properly.

"Come on!" Victor shouted.

"Did you finish with the castle?" I asked.

"It's ready, let's go!" he cried out even more tensely.

"And what about these?" I pointed at the High Council members.

"Fuck them!" he snarled out, "Come on!"

"Let me just free Dell and Conroy." I replied and turned to them.

"Leave them, there's no time!" he almost shouted.

Oops! My inner red light switched on. I stopped and looked at Victor. He had beads of sweat on his forehead. His eyes were wandering around.

"What's going on?" I asked.

I didn't reply, just looked at the door behind him worriedly.

My eyes fell on the Council members. How did I not notice it before? They were all looking absent and indifferent. Their eyes were blank. They didn't move. Saliva was dripping from their mouths. They were all drugged!

I felt the electricity going through my body again.

I hear boots rattling.

Elizabeth burst into the room. In a camouflage uniform. With a gun in her hands. Heading a company of troopers.

Come on, now, stories with unexpected ending?

She looked first at me, and then at Victor:

"Why is he still alive?"

Her voice was sharp and cruel. Her gaze reminded me of a keen machine-gunner. I did mention she was holding one of those, right? Or that she was ahead of a trooper squad?

Victor lowered his head. That was a surprise. Elizabeth took a deep breath and shouted at him:

"Did you fall for him, too, you stupid fag?"

Hey, look at that!

Elizabeth cracked her neck (I don't know why, but I didn't like it at all) and said angrily:

"Do I have to do everything alone?"

She lifted the machine-gun and accepted the resignation of the entire High Council – quickly, cruelly and once and for all. Drugged as they were, I doubted they even understood what happened to them.

On the one hand, that was good, because it hurt less.

On the other hand…To kill someone without giving them the chance to know they were about to die…is nasty, vicious and disgusting!

I felt pure hatred towards the blue-eyed blond beauty. I wished I would leave my mark on that pretty skin of hers. By using two knives, that is!

She glanced at me, clenched her teeth and hissed:

"What, you can't believe your eyes, is that it? You don't believe women are capable of leadership? You think we are only good for fucking, cooking and taking care of the children, is that it? Well, I have a surprise for you, asshole! Women are better than men in every single way!"

She was looking at me mockingly. I shrugged:

"I agree you can do many things. I agree you are fit to be leaders," I reached slowly in my pocket, took out a packet of cigarettes and lit one. "I agree that men only think they are in charge of things or do anything in particular even. I agree you are the ones who fuck us, not the other way round. I agree you make the World go round. And that's why," I blew the smoke in the most disdainful manner I could come up with, "and that's why it's in that wretched state!"

She clenched her teeth and Dalloway smiled. She cast a quick glance to him, then turned to me:

"People find you charming, huh?"

"Come near and I'll show you." I replied.

She smiled happily and spat:

"Men are such simple and dumb creatures! You want to fornicate even when death is at your door! You're just like animals! You act on instincts! Nothing more!"

I felt my hatred growing stronger and stronger. I snarled out:

"You're such a confused and unhappy woman."

She goggled her eyes at me. I went on:

"Apparently, you've never met a real man. You encountered only weak and good for nothing."

She was listening attentively:

"You've been fucked wrong." I added.

She slightly lowered the machine-gun. I could feel the rage rising. Once more I blew out the smoke in her direction and murmured:

"If you come to me, you'll never think of other guys again!"

She was silent.

"I'm not sure about one thing, though," I went on thoughtfully "you act just like a man. I wonder-"

She was looking attentively at me. All the others froze. I didn't spot a single dirty smile, nor a single burst of laughter. Apparently, she was great authority to them:

"I wonder-" I went on, fixing her gaze, "if you act like a man, shouldn't I throw you on that table on your stomach," she shivered "tear up all your clothes, twist your arms in the back..." she was panting, "and put it hard in your ass, just burst your pretty asshole open!"

She stopped breathing; she was just staring at me.

Nobody said anything. Nobody was able to breathe, even! Great discipline, if I may add!

I was holding the knife behind my back.

Elizabeth smiled and said with a trembling voice:

"You know me well," she shook her head "too well! No! I can't let you live!"

I threw the knife at her as she was saying it. I was aiming at her right shoulder, but hit her between the eyes. With the heft, though. She was already aiming and managed to pull the trigger. I was leaping behind of the portable medical equipment cabinet, formerly belonging to the late Borgia.

Bullets happily splashed on the carpet and the cabinet. Quickly and naughtily – just like a student, sneaking behind a helpful school-girl.

They stopped – there was no point of wasting the bullets. I took advantage of that and shouted mockingly:

"This birthday party is taking too long, don't you think?"

"You're the birthday boy," Elizabeth shouted back, "and we all want to congratulate you very much!"

Chapter 14 - Grand Finale

“Shoot first and ask questions not at all”.

Richard Marcinko

I heard steps. Quite a lot of them. They were coming from my left. Across the room, by the door at least three men were holding me at gun-point, in case I showed up behind the cabinet. I looked at Tanaka’s corpse, lying face down, next to the table with the late High Council. My knife was sticking out of his neck.

I wondered how fast I can crawl.

And why didn’t I have the Vision?

It seemed I was on my own.

Again.

The minute I saw a muzzle behind the left corner of the cabinet, I bent down with all the selflessness I could gather, and threw myself towards Tanaka like a wild-cat at its prey, pulled out the knife from his neck (it was my knife after all, and he wouldn't need anymore) and dived under the table like a gigantic rat.

You'll say I exposed myself to the bullets in a very stupid way.

I'll argue that someone might have hit me anyway. So, it was better to do something about it than to squat behind the cabinet, holding my balls in hand.

In the same moment when I leaped from behind the cabinet, the guys by the door opened fire. That was why I dove under the table, after picking up the knife. I could still hear the shooting and impact of bullets on various surfaces. They were hitting the table, the carpet, some of the late High Councilors. I crawled under the table knowing very well it was just a temporary measure; very soon someone would kneel and hit me from below. I crawled out on the right between two members of the Council. Still bending, I dashed to the other end the table. A second before I reached it, I stood up. I saw three people at the door, waiting for me. How sweet and kind of them! I leaped to the right. Now the three lined up and was standing to the left of the one closest to the left. While he was turning to see where I went, with one giant leap I landed next to him. I grabbed his gun, pointing at me, drew it closer and banged my head on the guy's head, thus sending him unconscious to the floor. The second soldier received a kick in the chest and a one-ticket to the floor as well. I didn't pay attention to the third one, but jumped through the door.

After I went through the door, I immediately glued myself to the wall.

The first one arrived on a silver platter. He basically begged me to shoot him in the face. After that I decided they weren't worth waiting for, so I started showing my head and firing at irregular intervals at my moving targets.

There was nothing else they could do except go for cover as much as they could and wait for my bullets to run out. Unless they had a back up on its way.

However, I was wrong. Elizabeth turned out to be an even nastier bitch than I thought.

"Hey, wise guy," she shouted "why don't you have a look at your friends!"

She meant Dell and Conroy.

"Okay," I shouted back, "don't shoot!"

I carefully peeked with one eye. With my right eye. Elizabeth was standing by the metal grates where Dell and Conroy were tied down. Dalloway was standing by her side, pointing a machine-gun at them. Elizabeth was holding something long in her hand. She was looking at me viciously:

"It's a ramrod," she shook the iron "Victor will shoot them if you decide to be a hero. And guess where I am about to tuck this ramrod in, if you don't come here in five?"

I hid back behind the corner.

"I'm not kidding and I'm not waiting for you to make up your mind," Elizabeth shouted, "One,"

I showed up abruptly, fired at her and Dalloway, then at the rest of the troopers. I hit two soldiers right away. I had always thought I was wrong to choose the doctor's profession – I should've become a butcher, it feels more like me. I dashed in the room to the soldiers with my gun pointing at them. Two of them fell to the floor themselves; I had to help the rest do the same. I kicked one of the guys on the floor in the head; the other got the best of my buttock.

I think Elizabeth and Dalloway were shooting at me at that time.

I felt a kick in my left shoulder, which threw me on my back to the floor. I rolled over. I couldn't feel my left arm, and my shoulder was hurting like hell. Tears came out.

I got hit by a bullet, I thought. It was better to lie still. Elizabeth and Dalloway ran to me. Lying on my right side, I opened fire. I took Elizabeth down. I hit her in the chest and she fell back. Dalloway threw himself on the floor. I pointed the gun at his forehead in the same moment when he pressed his gun at mine. We pulled the triggers simultaneously. Click! We were both out of bullets.

Sometimes you just have bad days.

We stood up one against each other – only two feet between us. I looked at my shoulder – it was bleeding badly. It was bleeding more than my two wrists, my left armpit and my left thigh. Fortunately, the bullet had hit only the back part of the deltoid muscle. It could have been worse.

Dalloway shook his head:

"I really like you and I didn't want things to go that far!"

"If you're waiting for me to bleed to death," I replied "I'll kill you long before that!"

"Have you always been such a prick?" he seemed curious.

"Yeah," I replied seriously "have you always been a traitor?"

He puckered his brows and the corners of his mouth frowned:

"That's my calling!"

He took out his army knife and attacked me. He was quick, experienced and unscrupulous. I didn't want to move my left hand – it was restraining and stiffening my body. The fight was causing my numerous wounds to bleed even more. Well, if it was going to be a critical day, let it really be so to its full extent.

After the first attack we withdrew from each other. We were panting, sweaty, and dirty. Dirty from the inside, as well as the outside.

I said panting;

"Tell me what was that all about?"

"We redistributed the power," he answered, also panting, "now we are above all else in the Organization."

"You?" I was surprised.

"Elizabeth and me," he cleared it out.

I looked at her – she was lying on her back. There was no blood on the chest where the bullet had hit her. Fuck, she was wearing a bullet-proof vest! When shall I stop being so dumb and start learning from my mistakes?

Victor grinned at me:

"We've made a court take-over, so to say, and you came in handy. It's true you're headstrong and didn't do exactly what you were supposed to, but you did something right, anyway."

Now it was my turn to attack. A push to the chest, a slice at the stomach, blocking the knife Victor was swaying at me, a punch to his stomach, a feint up to his throat, and then I cut his left armpit and retreated.

He also retreated and looked at his arm – it was bleeding profusely – he transferred his knife to his left hand and grinned:

"You never stop, do you?" he pointed at my left shoulder with his knife. "We'll never be even!"

"I think you're right!" I replied and attacked again.

Honestly, we were fighting so fiercely, sparkles flew out of our knives.

A feint upwards, a block on the side, then in the middle, a step on the left, a twist, a bend to avoid his stroke to my neck, then I cut him on the left foot and retreat. He looks at me without pain or fear, only bloodlust in his eyes. A true warrior!

"Soon our wounds will be even!" I shouted.

"Fuck you!" he snarled out.

"Is it worth it," I asked him, blocking three stabs and one stroke to my neck, "dying in the name of a rotten idea and a sick pornographic society? Dying in the name of this stinking Organization?"

"I have nowhere else to go!" he attacked fiercely, "I can't go back!" he retreated to the right, so that he could punch me with his left hand and attacked again, "I have nothing left! I have no choice!"

I blocked a stab in the stomach, stepped to the right and with a kick I smashed his left knee. He roared and fell on the left. He tried to cut my leg, while he was falling, but I pulled back:

"I have a proposition for you." I said.

"Why don't you shove it up your ass!" he hissed.

"Come with me to prison."

"Fuck you!" he snarled out in helpless malice.

I shook my head, and then asked:

"Where's the remote for the explosives?"

"Go to hell!" he snapped.

I sighed. I stepped on his left hand and took away his knife. He tried to push my aside with kicks and with his right, badly-cut arm. I punched him hard three times in the face. He calmed down. I searched his pockets and found the remote. I confiscated it and put it in my front pocket.

Then I stood up and looked around.

Dell and Conroy! I stumped along to the metal grates. I didn't know that it was so difficult to walk with an injured thigh! I came to the grates. They were about a feet high and made of strong edgy iron sticks. Those poor bastards! They were covered in wounds. They could barely moan! I could terror and incredible suffering in their eyes. They were tied down with some cables. I started cutting them with my knife. In that moment I heard a familiar blond blue-eyed female voice, full of nasty promises, behind my back.

"Wise guy, throw away the knife!"

I let go of the knife.

"Turn around!"

As I turning around, I took out the explosives remote and switched it on. I only had to press this other button and…I turned around.

Elizabeth was standing with legs wide-spread, disheveled, sweaty and mean, aiming the gun at me. She smiled with a touch of superiority:

"What did you think? That you've won? You'll never learn!"

"That's what my friends keep telling me," I shrugged.

"You have no idea how long I had to wait for this moment!" she enunciated, "Killing the High Council, those old motherfuckers! To finish off the old fag and his dumb bastard! To bring all the Organization's resources under my sway! To conquer the World and do whatever I like!"

I shook my head. I kept bleeding. To die of blood loss, while I was listening to the rattling of a sick twisted woman? Wasn't that dumb and ironic or...was it punishment?

Waving the remote, I pointed at the tied down, tortured and bleeding Carter Dell and Alistair Conroy.

"Do you consider this a fair price for the winning?"

She smiled beastly:

"A fair one, even a low one!"

I raised the remote:

"Do you know what this is?"

She smiled.

"That's a one-way ticket to the express train to the Other Side." I elucidated.

"You wouldn't dare!" she hissed (she was better at this than Dalloway), "You'll die too!"

"We are all going to die some day," I could feel the result of the blood loss – my strength was leaving me, "someone will day of a bullet, another will drown, some will get hit by a car, others will have heart attacks, somebody else will just go to sleep and never wake up… What 's the difference? Why wait until we're old and grey?" I raised my eyebrows.

She was considering the possibilities. I was almost decided to end it all here and now.

"Don't!" Elizabeth almost shouted "Come with me!"

"I already had this conversation with Borgia and Tanaka," I explained "One had a knife in the neck; the other didn't have a neck to brag about at all. What would you choose?"

"Don't," she lowered her gun "Please, don't. Come, I'll take you away from the castle and I'll help you get better."

"What about them?" I pointed at Conroy and Dell.

"I'll take them too!"

"Free them and let's go!" I ordered; I was getting dizzy. "Who were those suits who flew here with Little Hans?"

She came and started to untie the captives. She looked at me wryly and explained:

"These men are governmental representatives from all over the world."

"What?"

"In order to preserve their power and influence, they used our services," she was cutting the cables with her army knife, "Now it was our turn to call them up and assign them tasks. That's how they become ours. In that way, their governments will become ours. And their countries will become ours. Forever!"

She freed Carter Dell and he sat on the grate, moaning and groaning. I barely recognized him under the bruises and cuts.

"You sick bitch!" he moaned.

"Shut up, Dell!" I asked politely.

My strength was seriously weakening. I felt really dizzy.

Victor Dalloway stood up with difficulty. He saw Elizabeth cutting Conroy's cables and exclaimed:

"You stupid bitch! Are you changing sides again?"

"Shut up, you little faggot!" she hissed as cornered cobra, ready to strike.

"I may be a faggot, but I did my job, right?"

"Yes!" she replied "You did your job, now get lost!"

"Let's not go there, sweetie," Dalloway bent down to get a machine-gun from one of his dead colleagues. "Don't do that!"

She waited for him to stand up and hissed warningly:

"Don't push me, Victor! Leave while you can!"

"I can't stop pushing," he said with a smile, "you know I have to!"

He aimed the gun at her. She slightly bent down and with a single elusive move she threw the knife at him. She got him straight in the wind-pipe. He looked at her with surprise, let go of the gun, reached the knife, then looked at me with extreme pain and grief in his eyes and ...fell down.

Look at that – she was really fast and effective!

She looked at me wryly; now I could see an entirely different creature in her eyes. The kind psychologist, flirting with me in prison, was just a figment of my imagination. She had never existed. That thing before me was a ruthless creature. A cold, calculating creature without a hint of hesitation or humaneness.

Okay, now I feel free.

My vision was blurring. The blood loss was doing its thing; I didn't have much time left. I was about to die anyway, so at least I wanted to do this one thing. I intended to blow up the castle. With everyone in it.

But before that I wanted to get Dell and Conroy out of this place. I decided they had come to their senses and deserved to live.

Elizabeth took out another knife and freed Conroy. He also sat on the grate with a moan. She helped them step on the floor.

"We are leaving." I announced.

Elizabeth went first, I was behind her, Dell and Conroy were in the back. She led us through corridors and staircases all the way to the castle's antechamber. I was swaying as if I was drunk, Dell and Conroy were leaning on each other, limping and groaning. They were naked but they didn't care. It you were them, you wouldn't care whether you were on *Big Brother*. As you remember, the castle had a large main entrance with iron doors, then a hall with two side entrances and a smaller entrance with wooden doors and iron plated, leading to the enormous ball-room. We found ourselves in the hall with two side entrances. I halted and glanced at the ball-room. The party was at its peak – wining and dining, and a lot of dancing.

"Who are they?" I asked Elizabeth.

"They are just pets," she shrugged "Gofers. Easily replaceable and always at our disposal."

I nodded and looked at her with all seriousness, no words needed.

She shivered and looked down.

"Don't make me go in there. Please."

"Why should let you live?" I asked.

"What would you gain from my death?" she murmured with trembling voice.

"Nothing!" I splattered. "I haven't profited from anybody's death. I always had to give something of mine!"

She was shivering. I was weak and wounded. My blood was pouring out of my body. I had my foot on the Other Side. But she wasn't a fool. She knew I could kill her before she even moved.

"I want one thing from you!" I said with difficulty.

"Whatever you say!" she looked at me as my faithful dog.

"I'm dying," I swayed "Promise to this dying man that you'll change and wouldn't harm anybody from on!"

She looked down.

"Is that so hard?" I was amazed.

She was silent. I stumped to one of the walls and leaned on it. I was about to collapse, but I knew I shouldn't.

"If I promise you that," she whispered "I'll have to keep that promise."

"Of course, you'll have to!" I insisted.

She was considering it.

"What do you want from this life?" I asked.

She raised her head in surprise.

"What do you want from it?" I repeated.

She looked at me with sheer astonishment. I shook my head:

"Get lost!"

"Come with me!" she begged.

"Get lost!" I repeated threateningly.

She stepped backwards to the entrance. Her gaze was rather strange. Really strange. Dell and Conroy were limping far away.

I gathered all the strength I had left, and pushed away from the wall. I stepped in the middle of the hall and looked at the remote in my hand.

I looked inside the ball-room. How did Elizabeth put it? Gofers. What about the children running around? They were supposed to follow their parents' footsteps…

And what about me?

My story ends here.

I was doing only things that weighed down on me lately. It was about time I stopped!

Was that my assignment in this world? To stop the viciousness in this castle? And to go with it?

I think too much!

I closed my eyes. I thought, *'Forgive me, Lord, and take me.'* Then I pressed the button on the remote. I heard a series of strong explosions right away. I opened my eyes. The people in the ball-room were running to and fro, looking at the crumbling walls. The blasts were getting louder. The earth was shaking. People finally reacted properly and ran to the exit. They were pushing, crushing, and smashing each other – like a herd of wild boars. They were running straight at me.

They were going to crush me.

The blasts frequented. Look at Victor, he was really good! God rest his soul.

The lamps went out. A large stone block, then another, then another were falling at the exit of the ballroom and were cutting off the way out. To die under the stones in the dark in fear and terror! A bad kind of death!

Am I the one causing all that?

Who am I?

The ceiling cracked above me. Dust was falling on my head.

Please, Lord, take me.

A blow on the head…

Apparently, God didn't want me just yet.

I opened my eyes. I was lying on one side in the back seat of a car. I looked around. Elizabeth was sitting beside me and was watching me with care and concern.

The driver noticed I was conscious and exclaimed grumpily:

"I didn't think I had to save scoundrels besides lost souls!"

The voice sounded familiar. The driver turned round and smiled at me. It was the prison Priest! I didn't have the strength to express my astonishment.

Elizabeth stroked me gently on the forehead.

I looked at her doubtfully.

What do you think? Can a former 100 % bitch, totally ruthless and unscrupulous, with immoral behavior could change and become…a good woman?

I sighed and closed my eyes.

I will trust her.

If she lies to me, I'll cut her open!

And then I might marry her.

I wonder what she thinks about it.

I'll wait. Time will tell.

"Hey, father," I said weakly.

He turned to me again.

"I decided to follow your advice," I said even more weakly (Elizabeth was stroking me on the forehead), "I decided to start from a scratch…anew…"

He smiled at me. Elizabeth also smiled at me. Well, I had to smile back, didn't I?

From a scratch. And that was it.

Full stop.

Comma.

Did I mention that the Priest was actually a high-ranking officer of the Secret Services?

I didn't?

That's strange!

I've missed it…somehow…

Now Elizabeth and I are doing time in a liberal regime prison. In separate prisons, of course. We are learning how to be civilized people. And how to contact normally with people.

Why are we in liberal regime prisons, you may ask? Well, because "we cooperated in disclosing, locating and eradicating an extremely dangerous international organization of criminal elements."

It's a very interesting interpretation of the recent events, don't you think?

The Priest came up with this interpretation. And said it To Whom It May Concern. With the respective superlatives regarding Elizabeth and me.

Sometimes you just can't cope without some help from others.

Now, Elizabeth and I pay ourselves weekly visits. Sometimes she comes to my prison, sometimes I do to her. It's like long-distance dating, ha ha!

It's weird what a Priest can do. He promised us that when we get out, he'll marry us…if we behave. Or else, he'll shoot us dead personally!

Aren't we aiming too high?

We'll see.

And now, about the Vision I used to have. Sometimes I still have it. Not very often. Only in critical situations. No one can explain what or why. I'm a little worried that Borgia used to have it too….

I have a feeling this story isn't over yet.